the happy pigs

the happy pigs
lucy harkness

A NOVEL

St. Martin's Minotaur
New York

www.minotaurbooks.com

ISBN 0-312-28286-9

Library of Congress Cataloging-in-Publication Data
Harkness, Lucy, 1969–
    The happy pigs / Lucy Harkness.
        p. cm.
    ISBN 0-312-28286-9
    1. Police—England—London—Fiction. 2. London (England)—
Fiction. 3. Policewomen—Fiction. I. Title.
  PR6058.A6866 H36 2002
  823'.914—dc21   2001048595

First published in Great Britain by The Blackstaff Press Limited

First St. Martin's Minotaur Edition: January 2002

10 9 8 7 6 5 4 3 2 1

For Ian

the happy pigs

Contemporaneous notes

not entirely sure how to do this ...

hot bath cold beer hot bath cold beer hot bath cold beer hot bath cold beer and I'm repeating this to myself until it is completely meaningless, a chanting mantra to keep my head together as long as it takes to get into the tube station through the people through the hot pre-breathed air through the barrier down the escalator onto the platform, hot bath cold beer hot bath cold beer and I might as well be concentrating on cold bath hot beer for all the good it is doing but on I go, mind the gap, get in get on get home, why can't this work now this always gets me through? hot bath hot bath hot bath cold beer, stand in the middle of the carriage so as to be in position to slip into a seat as soon as someone gets off but look there's a nice man letting me sit down, shit I must look like shit, quick check for bloodstains, mudstains, maybe he's just being nice, shit I am in a bad way, concentrate, hot bath cold beer hot bath cold beer, not counting the stops but only three to go, bag over shoulder, tube pass in hand, hot bath cold beer running in my head, this could be a normal bad day, hot bath cold beer, and up and off and let the escalator carry me home, let the tide of rush hour wash me onto the street, will this little hand ever be clean? hot bath should do the trick, key in door, hi Margaret, no answer, good, drop bag feed cat open fridge select cold beer run hot bath clothes in wash, powder, power, hey I'm not usually this organised, the back bit of my head must have been working this out all the way home. Step into bath. And ... re ... lax.

The hot-bath-and-cold-beer thing started at uni. Actually, in those days I'd have had a joint as well, but obviously, what with the job and so on, I can't really keep dope in the house any more. It worked when dearJon left me for an older woman with money (even I could see that made sense but I've always said, I'd rather be sensitive than logical) and it worked when my philosophy tutor said I was the worst student he'd had in twenty-seven years of teaching. OK, so this is a fairly large crisis but quite frankly I have to get a grip. I don't have a choice here, I can't just fall apart, feel sorry for myself, give up or break down ... more bubbles, more steam and more beer.

Wipe a face-cloth width of steam off the bathroom mirror and look at my face for a minute – I'm flushed, bright-eyed, hectic. I almost look drunk. I don't look like myself at all. I look wide awake, alive, kind of excited. I recognise the look I get from skiing too fast on unfamiliar slopes, driving too fast on country roads, and as the mirror steams over again I turn out the light and climb back into the bath in the dark. I don't want to face myself with that face on. It is not a face for public view. I look as if I've just won a race, or had an amazing shag. No visible marks or scars, that's the main thing. No obvious scratches or bruises to explain away.

There are a couple of important things that I have to do before I can think about what happened this evening. I have to get Candy through her trial, I have to get my annual appraisal over with, convincing the new boss who starts tomorrow that I need to move into another department, and I have to sort out my love life – what am I saying? I need to get a love life – and work out what to do about my warring Irish parents. I need to stop feeling guilty over my depressive ex-boyfriend, Keith, and I need to decorate the house, get fit, have a holiday, get out of London. Then, maybe, I can work out how to pick up a Get Out of Jail Free card ... There have been stages in my life where I've had the time to sit and think and sort out my head, it's just that this month isn't one of them.

Let's face it, there have been times in my life when I did nothing but think, not very good thoughts, not very good times, times when there was just no satisfactory answer to the basic why. But eventually I stopped living entirely in my head and tried living in my body occasionally – taking care of it, exercising it, even pampering it from time to time – so now, although deep down I am aware of the essential futility of everything, I can always put things to the back of my mind and occupy the front with a yoga- or swimming-induced feeling of calm. Calm is something I have been steadily working towards, and one day I will be good at it.

The only thing I've ever been really good at was one summer when I had a job driving tractors on a farm in Kent, doing the potato harvest and bale-carting, and all that. I was a great tractor driver, but sadly the career opportunities were lacking and I headed back to town when the autumn came.

And I'm a good waitress too. I can do all that taking-bookings-while-carrying-four-plates and no-ticing which tables need clearing and reminding chef that the woman on six is allergic to dairy products stuff while smiling at the right people to ensure a large tip, but in the end I realised that if I was going to work silly hours and deal with awkward people every day, I might as well get a decent wage for it, and looked for better paid employment.

I was never that good as a uniformed constable – not patient enough, I suppose, not really concerned enough about other people's problems. That's OK if you're a bloke, of course, but even in the police force – oops, that should be police service – women are expected to lend a sympathetic ear to every tale of woe, soothe and calm every hysterical runaway, pick up the drunks and rescue the waverers on high bridges. Well, I lived with someone for five years who was always threatening to kill himself, so maybe that inured me to similar scenes at work. I'm not saying I was needlessly harsh. I mean, I gave everyone a chance, lent people money to get home, drove lost and confused elderly persons round in the hope they'd recognise where they lived, called out social services and ambulances where and when required. But it is a great relief to get out of uniform, so that you are no longer so obviously at everyone's beck and call, owned by the taxpaying public at large.

And, of course, while you are in uniform, everyone you meet thinks you're stupid, because if you had a brain you'd be in CID. Or doing a proper job. OK, so from time to time you'd get a good job in – a stolen credit card, or a possession of drugs with intent to supply, or a bagful of forged fifty-pound notes – but someone else would always step in and take it over and that would be the last you'd hear of it. And no one ever says, thanks, that was a good job, well done.

Part of a chain, alienated from the end product, you could say.

You can spend thirty years chasing shoplifters and taking them to court over a tenner's worth of chocolate or a couple of books, nicking drunks for being disorderly or incapable, crossing people for public order offences and poor people for begging, breathalysing motorists, and so on and so forth – many people do and I'm not saying there's anything wrong with that – it is just, when I was doing all that, I thought there were more interesting ways to pass the time, bigger fish to angle after. So now I'm stressed out and at the end of my tether, contemplating putting in a request to go back to the easy life. Well, easier, anyway.

One of the things I am pretty good at is taking statements. Not nearly as easy as people think. If they tell you their story back to front with bits added on at the end and a few contradictions here and there, as they almost always do, you still have to turn it into a coherent, reasonable whole. I turn up, sit down, ask a few questions, get patronised by some fat middle-class woman who thinks her daughter's the only person ever to get groped on the tube and assumes I must be stupid because I'm only a police officer not something expensive in the city. I don't get annoyed. I am appropriately concerned, although, of course, being a mere police officer, I could never understand how the poor sensitive darling feels. At the end of an hour and a half (I'm quick and fluent but sometimes I have to go slow, so they think they're getting their taxpayers' money's worth) I leave with all the information I need to identify the assailant, prove the offence and convince the court that this particular case is indeed a nasty attack. I know the right things to say and the right way to say them. I can even spell quite difficult words, which surprises a lot of people.

How about: 'Try and go into as much detail as you can, the more you remember now, the less you'll have to think about it in the future ... We can make it into a complete story and you'll feel it's at a distance from you. We'll get it out of your head and onto the statement paper – that way you won't have to try and remember because it'll all be here in black and white when you go to court.'

Well, if only it was that simple. Here I am trying to do the same thing for myself and I know I'll go round the issue so often it'll be wrapped and buried and concealed in no time. The gaps where the walls used to be have been papered over, with pictures and colours and textures so fine, as I wrote in my first year logic exam.

How about: 'It's not your fault, nobody has the

right to do that to you. Think about it, you'd never do that to a stranger/loved one/child, would you? Well then, how can you let them get away with doing it to you?'

How about: 'Don't start to feel sorry for him, you're the victim in this. He knew he had a wife and family and job and mortgage when he attacked you – he's the one putting them at risk, not you.'

How about this: I'm supposed to uphold the queen's peace and protect life and limb. Serve the public. Still, that must include me somewhere along the line. Everyone has the right to defend themselves, it is as basic as that. And, anyway, I haven't got time to think about it now.

Problem: too large to go into now.

Solution: sort out all other top priority problems (see above) and hope it goes away in the meantime.

The main thing is Candy: she's ten years old, she's been kidnapped, raped and tortured, she's been through it all in court once already and the man who did it has sacked his defence and the trial is starting all over again. I'm her chaperone. I pick her up and drive her to court. I did the initial video statement along with her social worker and I've spent the last year at the beck and call of her dreadful mother and dreadful stepfather, who are only too glad to have a free babysitter and would lumber me with the other four kids given half a chance. The other four being permanently enraged and jealous because of the extra attention Candy is getting. Never mind that she's incontinent and can't sleep alone; never mind that she's terrified of strangers and whimpers at loud noises; never mind that she's a tiny child who looks more like an eight-year-old – her siblings are still pissed off because she gets taken out for the day now and then courtesy of my DCI, who seems to think that children can get over anything if you just feed them enough McDonald's.

So all in all it wouldn't help her one bit if I disappeared or resigned or whatever. I'm stuck with her and she does seem to trust me, even if she doesn't think much of the way I dress. (Not enough glitter.) She'll need looking after for years, and I'm the only volunteer for it so far. The trial should start this week and barring accidents/further manipulations by the defendant, it should be all over within ten days or so. Apparently he's going to defend himself. Shitbag. Hope he tells the court what he said to the chap who arrested him – 'she loved it; it was her idea, I tell you, she was gagging for it', et cetera, et cetera. (Lovely, she is, only ten years old but has the body of an eight-year-old.)

Men really are revolting, I think, but some of them hide it better than others.

Some of the first interview I did with Candy has been made into part of the training package now – they use it for people doing the new child protection course. There's a passage in the transcript where Candy's saying about the bad man putting a thing into her bottom and it really hurting and I ask, what thing? And the social worker says to me, for God's sake, I think we all know what thing, and Candy says, no, not his willy but a spike thing. And when the Central Operations Unit boys did another search of his house they found a home-made torture instrument, a kind of modified cattle-prod thing with a couple of nails in the end, lovingly crafted and fully adaptable, plug-in or battery operated, hidden round the bend in the chimney.

One of the Central Ops boys asked if he could have it when the trial is over.

See what I mean about men being pigs?

(How does a paedophile know when it's bed-time? The big hand touches the little hand.)

Sorry if I sound at all hysterical, but I have had rather a bad day.

Evidence gathering:
initial statements

NB: CRIMINAL DAMAGE ACT 1971, SECTION 1
*Don't knacker something if it isn't yours, unless,
of course, you think the owner wouldn't mind.*

OK, so if I were taking my statement about today it
would start like this:

Statement of LOUISA BARRATT
Age OVER 21

Occupation DETECTIVE CONSTABLE

This statement consisting of ————— pages
each signed by me is true to the best of my
knowledge and belief and I make it knowing
that if tendered in evidence I shall be liable to
prosecution if I have wilfully stated anything
which I know to be false or do not believe to
be true.

Which, by the way, is standard police language;
you probably need an above average IQ to work out
what it means. You certainly need to be pretty
smart to work out the new caution, which strikes
me as funny, really, since most of the people who
get cautioned wouldn't be in that position if they
were anywhere near smart. Then again, their so-
licitors usually understand it, and at the end of the
day the actual suspect or offender isn't that important in the whole process, playing a fairly minor
role in the proceedings.

'You do not have to say anything but it may harm
your defence if you do not mention when questioned something you later rely on in court. Anything you do say may be given in evidence.'

Try and say it out loud ... that way it makes
sense.

'You do not have to say anything' *pause* 'but it
may harm your defence' *pause* 'if you do not mention' *emphasise the last three words* 'when questioned
something you later rely on in court' *pause*

'anything you do say may be given in evidence.'

Whenever you start a taped interview with someone you are supposed to ascertain that they fully understand the caution, what it means in theory and how it affects them in the present instance. So there you are, sitting not terribly comfortably in a small soundproofed interview room, usually badly lit and painted a dark magnolia, overheated and stuffy and stale, furnished with a desk, four or five chairs, a tape recorder, a metal wastepaper bin doubling as an ashtray, and a typed sheet of procedural requirements stuck to the desk – the cheat sheet, it is called, it reminds the interviewing officer to caution the suspect, give the special warnings where necessary, state the time and date at the start, all those details you can so easily forget. There are always torn bits of cellophane from the tape wrappers on the floor, cigarette butts in the bin, burn marks on the edges of the desk. A great setting to put people at their ease and encourage frank and open discussion of the offences under consideration.

Police Officer: So can you explain what the caution means in your own words and how it affects you in this particular case?

Suspect: Um, well, I don't have to say anything if I don't want to, yeah?

Pompous Male/Pushy Female Solicitor: I have discussed this with my client and am satisfied that he/ she understands the implications.

Always a pleasure, never a chore, dealing with the legal profession.

So, that statement.

I'm approaching this with a statement because I think I'm going to try and remember that I'm the victim in here – obviously the more people get to know this, the more likely it is that I'll end up answering questions having been cautioned. Hopefully not by someone I know; how embarrassing – like the last time I had a smear done at the family planning clinic, the doctor said, by the way we have some student doctors with us this week, would you mind if they sit in with us? And not really being in much of a position to argue, I said, oh, of course not, bring them in by all means. But I was worried about recognising one of them – maybe one of my brother's friends, or someone I'd dealt with at work. As if knowing the person would make it shameful somehow.

But no, they wouldn't make me talk about it to someone I work with, surely not.

Well then.

I did say that I might circle round the nitty gritty of it, didn't I? Sure, everyone is entitled to set the scene to some extent – a reply to a caution, for instance, can be as long as you like. If it seems relevant, put it in.

On Tuesday 15 July 1997, one of those swelteringly warm stifling-in-the-city days, I was at work in the Child Protection Unit on Euston Road from

1100 hrs. (Don't know why we don't just say 11 a.m. – one of those silly procedures you never bother to question.) As it was a whole day free for paper-work, admin and generally catching up with things, I was working on a number of enquiries. I spoke to several other members of the team throughout the day on the phone and to my immediate supervisor, DS Eliot, who was the only other person in the office that morning. I have been a police officer in London for six years, and in that time I have worked at several central police stations. (Note I say 'police officer' rather than 'policewoman', for some reason I find that word annoying. It makes you sound as if you're not really one thing or the other, a hybrid or an approximation of both.) I completed my CID course in May last year after working on a robbery squad for most of the previous year. I have been working on the Child Protection Unit for just over a year.

We had a meeting at lunch time in the canteen with Paula Mills and Heather Wilson, two fairly senior social workers from the Youth Policy Review team, after which I returned to the office. Social workers tend to have an inbuilt distrust of police officers, and not all of them manage to conceal it during meetings. They think we're harsh and un-caring. We say, no, looking after the elderly and the mad isn't a police job, show me a crime and I'll deal with it, show me a runaway child and I'll call you.

DS Eliot left the office at around 1530 and I

worked alone until about 1700 hrs, at which time I went out to walk around the area. My duties include working with underage prostitutes and to do this effectively I have had to build up a rapport with some of the older regulars.

At approximately 1725 hrs I met two working women on Eversholt Street and stopped to talk to them. The evening was still hot but there was the faintest suspicion of a breeze rustling the crisp packets and sweet wrappers in the doorways and corners. The roads were busy with crammed double decker buses trundling along, filthy delivery vans and suicidal cyclists weaving in and out, and the odd plush car or limo here and there. Despite the traffic fumes and the litter on the grimy streets, I was feeling quite pleased with the way the day had gone. The women I met are called Alison and Maria. I believe their full names are known to uniform officers locally.

Maria is originally from Scotland, she's about thirty, five feet seven, with long black hair. I've known her for three years, since I worked at King's Cross as a uniformed homebeat officer. She has an almost incomprehensible accent and talks slightly too loudly, as if she knows people don't always catch what she's saying. Alison is a plump blond with a permanently tired expression. She's an alcoholic and is usually worrying about whether the childminder is looking after her daughter properly while she's out working. I have known her for about a year. Both these women will know me as 'Louisa from the Child Protection team', but I wouldn't rely on either of them being able to confirm the precise time that we spoke. Or even the date. I would say that neither of them was exactly sober or drug-free at the time we met.

Although both were moving and speaking normally, they displayed signs of intoxication, with enlarged pupils and slightly glazed expressions. But then that's fairly standard for the area and time of day. After greeting them and chatting briefly about this and that, we began to talk about my area of interest. I asked if they had noticed any new faces on the street in the past week or so. I like to keep a close eye on my patch, but lately I have been overstretched with other duties and have been unable to spend as much time out and about as I would like. The conversation went along the following lines.

I said, 'I have been working mainly days recently, so you may have noticed I've not been around. What have I missed, what's going on?'

Maria said, 'You should be so lucky, d'you want to swap jobs? Can't remember the last time I knocked off at five.'

Alison said, 'If you don't count that German bloke last Friday ...'

Maria said, 'No, seriously, there's not a lot to tell you. There was a mention of a new girl from Devon, supposed to be twelve or thirteen, but I saw her

17

yesterday – that's twelve or thirteen stone, I'm not kidding. Michelle reckons she was the year above her at school, so she's at least eighteen or nineteen.'

I said, 'Who's Michelle?' and they both went into a lengthy and unflattering description of a girl I knew by sight.

Maria and Alison aren't friends of mine – they're unreliable, catty, often off their heads and occasionally violent, and, of course, they're always on the lookout for easier ways of making a quick bit of cash – but it is in their interests to cut down on competition and they've both got young kids themselves, so they will usually tell me if any teenage waifs end up trying to make a living selling themselves on their turf.

We talked about the weather, uncomfortably humid but not bad for business, and Alison asked me about one of the uniform constables she'd met the other day, a young man from Exeter from a religious family. I don't think he even knew what a prostitute was until he came to work at King's Cross, and I think he thinks he can save these fallen women by encouraging them towards God. I had to tell her that yes, PC Foster was very pretty, but no, he wasn't available and was in fact happily married, so far as I knew.

The conversation was winding down and I was just starting to think about going back up to the office to pick up my jacket and go home when we were approached by a man. I had not met this man before and I do not believe that Alison or Maria knew him, either. I would describe him as a white male, aged about forty-five to fifty, six feet two tall and of a fairly large build. I would say he was slightly overweight, but overall he was more muscular-looking than fat. He was clean-shaven, with dark hair greying at the sides and receding at the temples, with very dark eyebrows and a faint five o'clock shadow. He had pale skin, as if he rarely went outdoors, oily-looking on the forehead and nose, and a long oval face. His eyes were dark, either dark grey or brown, with heavy pouches under them. I noticed when he was shouting in my face later on that they were slightly bloodshot, particularly in the inside corners. Despite the heat, the man was wearing a dark grey suit with a white shirt and a patterned tie, I think it had a yellow background and the pattern was of small squares in different colours. He wore black slip-on shoes, recently polished, and his appearance was tidy and quite smart – his clothing looked well cut and therefore probably expensive. He did not have any visible marks or scars and I do not remember seeing any jewellery other than a silver-coloured watch on his right wrist. The watch had a grey face and was analogue rather than digital. I did not recognise the make but it looked expensive.

I will refer to this man as Mr Suit.

Mr Suit came up to us as we stood chatting on the corner of Eversholt Street and Lancing Street. I was wearing a short grey pinstripe skirt, a white V-neck silk top and a pair of flat-heeled black loafers. I am five feet eight and of a slim to medium build. I had my hair done in a French plait, tucked under and clipped at the back and I was not wearing make-up. Alison was wearing a black Lycra skirt and matching cropped top, revealing her round white belly, with bare legs, bruised at the back of one knee, and scruffy white trainers. Maria wore a bright green dress, with black, clumpy-heeled shoes and a tatty green scarf wrapped round her long ponytail. Alison and Maria were both heavily made-up in a slapdash manner, more slap than dash, really. None of us signalled to him or spoke to him, he just approached us on the street corner for reasons known to himself and began to talk to us.

Mr Suit said, 'Afternoon, girls' and I noticed that he had a Midlands accent. He spoke quite loudly and seemed confident. Maria and Alison looked faintly embarrassed and neither replied. I saw no reason to speak to the man and so I turned on my heel, saying 'See you later' to the women.

I walked slowly back towards my office, not really thinking about anything, maybe planning an evening out with Margaret at the weekend, maybe just drifting along in a world of my own, until I was suddenly grabbed by the arm and swung round with some force. My assailant was Mr Suit. My hand moved instinctively to the inside pocket of the jacket I wasn't wearing to check for the collapsible baton I had clearly left in the office. An error a probationer would be ashamed to make. Mr Suit had a tight hold of my left upper arm, above the elbow, with his right hand. His left hand was raised threateningly towards my face. I glimpsed dark hair on the back of his hand and was about to shout at him to let go when he lowered his face to within an inch of mine and shouted at me.

This was in broad daylight on a busy street in an area I knew well and at this stage I was more annoyed than scared, although as he started to shout I became scared. He was six inches taller than me and very intimidating. He seemed very angry and was almost spitting his words out with rage. He said, 'So you think you can walk off on me. You must think you're really good, think you can pick and choose. Well, you'll see, I'm the one that picks and chooses. You'll all know me very soon.' All the while he was pulling me by the arm and I was trying to resist being pulled along towards a small weed- and rubbish-strewn entry alongside the Oceana Fish Bar. I could smell stale alcohol on him, also sweat and the remnants of some brand of aftershave I didn't recognise. I was desperately trying to attract the attention of a passerby, any passerby, but as usual the general public were busy seeing no evil, hearing no evil, as they rushed home from work or out to play. I had left my jacket in my office with my handy baton in it, my handcuffs were in my desk drawer, even my warrant card was two streets, three storeys and a corridor away. I suppose that at a glance we could have looked like a couple having a bit of a domestic, which seems to be an acceptable form of violence in this country.

Although it is a discipline offence to be on duty without the specified accoutrements, it is quite common practice to carry cuffs and stick on an as-and-when-required basis. There is no excuse for leaving one's warrant card behind. Unless one is going to Ireland. Although I always take mine with me to Ireland. The picture amuses my mother and we don't have much else to laugh about together.

A common error in statement-taking is that the police officer writing it all down will go to some lengths to set the scene and develop atmosphere, describing the people, places, sights, smells and so on, then set out the actual offence with something like 'and then he hit me twice, raped me and left'. This often happens because it is not easy to get people to talk about the awful things that happen to them, and, of course, it is embarrassing to talk about these awful things. Well, it's obvious really. Mrs Big House will talk all day about the charity shop she worked at, where she met Mr Care in the Community, but she won't want anyone reading the sordid details of what he put where, even if it is her civic duty to report the attack in case it happens to someone else.

I think if I were taking my statement about what happened today, I'd probably explain that the more detail I can manage now, the less questions there will be in court, should my case progress that far. But that would only be the case if I can keep on seeing myself as the victim in this. Of course, I am the victim in this.

So, what I need to do is write down every small detail and then I can put the paper away and get on with everything else important.

I have actually had a statement taken, years ago this was, when I was eighteen and had just left home, living in a big shared house, waitressing and housekeeping and generally getting by, hitching in and out of the town where I worked, which is why I had to make this statement, because I met the strange man hitching. It is funny, you know that hitching is dangerous, so you tell the bloke that your friends are watching from the house to see which car you get into and you don't realise that you're telling this stranger where you live. And if he happens to pass the front of your house most mornings, it becomes less like hitching and more like getting a lift from someone you know, and then one day your friend comes too and he learns your name, and then one night he's passing the pub as you leave to go home and again he offers and you don't even think twice – this is the bloke in the blue Renault, not some stranger, so in you get and he drops you to the door. Bit of a creepy bloke, but, hey, it saves the taxi fare. So you think it's weird when one of your housemates tells you they think they've seen the Renault parked across the road a few times lately, but you don't exactly worry about it. You think you'll mention it next time you see him, but the next time you see him it's nearly three in the morning. You've been drinking after hours with your friends who work in the pub and you're walking a zigzag route home without a care in the world, enjoying the silence and the clear cold night sky, when out of nowhere there are headlights in your face and a car engine and you just know it is the blue Renault, it has funny yellow-painted headlights, and your head suddenly clears and you know that it isn't coincidence or good luck that the man who always seems to turn up when you need a lift has just done it again. Half a mile to go; there's a ditch and then forest on either side of the road, no cars likely to pass. He's a fat old bloke but he's in a car, so running isn't going to work, unless you go into the trees, and, Christ, you don't believe this can really be happening, he gets out of the car and you're standing there in the headlights completely unable to make a decision and the back of your head says 'Beam me up, Scotty' but the front knows it's not funny, and before anything normal can happen to snap you out of this paralysis he just dives on you, a big bloke in a dark coat, and you're lying there in the road, for God's sake, squashed under this lump of a man and his scratchy face is in yours and he's so fat you can't move your arms, you couldn't push him off even if you could move your arms, and the only thing you can think of is that you could maybe bring a knee up fairly sharpish, but a part of your head you thought you'd left at home with your mum says, but that will hurt him! And that's it, that is funny, you break out of your dazzled-rabbit state and when he sticks his fat tongue in your mouth you bite it and bring that knee up as fast as you can in between his fat thighs, connecting just enough for him to jerk back, just enough for you to wriggle out and up and away into the trees. You know he won't follow and he doesn't. He shakes his head, you hope in pain, mumbles something and shuffles the few feet back to his car, door left open when he got out, dim light so you can see him reaching into the glove compartment, but you don't wait to see what he's looking for, you squirm through the undergrowth and hunch down and wait. As soon as the car moves off you're back on the road and running, following the rear lights round the bend towards the crossroads where you live. Surely he won't stop there and he doesn't, but even so, you skirt round the field and come in through the back, not turning the lights on, realising for the first time that all this has happened in complete silence, how bizarre, why didn't you shout?

And the next day you get up really early and walk to work and think how much you are going to enjoy this walk every morning in the safe bright daylight.

You don't go the police straightaway – why would you, you've never spoken to a police officer in your life, never known one and you don't exactly meet them socially, do you? And you know you shouldn't accept lifts from strangers and pretty soon you think you were probably asking for it and got off quite lightly really.

After a few days thinking about things you tell the rest of your household what happened and the boys are really upset and angry for you, so when they see the Renault parked up in town a week or so later they wait for the man but he doesn't come. So they trash it, kick in the yellow-painted headlights, scratch the blue paint, get carried away with the sheer destructive pleasure of it and pull off the wipers and bend the aerial into a tortured triangle and rip away the number plate you will never be able to forget, snap the wing mirrors and dent the doors. Of course, they are then arrested for causing criminal damage; of course they don't get away with it, although there is never a policeman there when you want one. So then you have to go to the police station and explain why your friends have done this, and the chap on the front desk doesn't believe you and you have to make a scene until someone else comes to sort you out and eventually it is easier for them to listen to you than keep on telling you to shut up and go away.

You finally make that fully detailed statement, with background detail and foreground detail and every greasy grey hair and pockmark noted for future reference, and your friends are bailed pending enquiries and you worry and they worry and eventually they are told that there will be no police action because the owner of the vehicle has declined to make a complaint about the damage.

You wonder what has happened to your statement, you wonder why you never hear from the police again, but then you say, well, it wasn't that important anyway. You don't want to have to see the man again, and letting it lie seems like the best option.

After a few years you tell people about it, you say, yeah, I had a kind of stalker once, but you think you've got over it. It's just you can't bear to be bear-hugged, you panic if someone presses suddenly or closely against you at a football game, you have an unreasonable fear of being cornered by large men. Though how can a fear of being cornered by large men be unreasonable, surely it's the most natural fear in the world, probably more important for survival than a fear of large growly animals or fear of fire. You are always aware that most of the people you live, work and socialise with are larger and stronger than you and could easily hurt you if they decided to. This is something you can live with, it is not exactly news, after all.

Then when you go back to your home town, study, get away again, this time to university, one of your year tutors is too pissed to walk home at the end of someone's party, so you try to help him and you and a mate are half-carrying, half-dragging him along because somehow he's lost control of his legs but his right hand seems to have a life of its own and, hey, here we go again, it must be something I'm doing wrong or not doing right, one person's friendly goodnight grope is another person's indecent assault, and there is a job and a family at stake here and you did push him away before anything seriously wrong happened, so least said, soonest mended. Now, with the benefit of hindsight, a few years older and much less naive, I'd have the man in a cell before he could say, 'Now about your exam results . . .'

I feel as if I have seen it all, I have dealt with it all, and so nothing shocks me now. I remain calm and professional, at least outwardly, as I see and hear about the most appalling assaults and violations. I know that most of my women friends have received unwanted attention from various men at various times. I've been flashed at in one of those great, cosy, walled-in only-one-way-in-and-out booths in an Irish pub by a very drunk middle-aged man, I've been flashed at in the street by an Arab with a huge yellow sideways-bending dick, I've been rubbed up against on a rush-hour train and propositioned on the tube and the really amazing thing, the truly unbelievable thing, is quite how everyday-normal all this is. Other women think it's funny that I get so outraged by what are, after all, everyday events.

Men refuse to acknowledge that these things happen to everyone.

It is not just me.

It really is not just me.

I don't wear make-up unless I'm in a very bad mood. I don't dress outrageously without good cause. I keep my distance from the men I work with, men on the street, men on the tube. It isn't anything I'm doing wrong. The truth is, being female seems to be provocation enough sometimes. But having spent time with women, boys, girls like Candy, I can quite honestly say that I have been more harassed than hurt.

We all have our reasons for doing the job that we do: mine was, when I joined, that I wanted to get some of the flashers and gropers and rapists off the streets. I'd patrol those mean streets, eagle-eyed and merciless in the pursuit of wrong-doers and justice. Now I'm not so sure why I do this job. Which is why I need to see my new boss and request a transfer. So I can get my head together, find some new strength from somewhere, sort my life out.

Call that a slight diversion from the main body of the statement if you will, but I think it should stay in, part of the background information, in a way, and vital mitigation for what is yet to come. Not sure how to go on with this, though.

Maybe tomorrow I'll get there ... it'll be easier in the morning.

Investigation:
identification procedures

NB: CRIMINAL LAW ACT 1967
*This Act abolished felonies. Hurrah! cried felons all
around the country. One such misdemeanour was
the wonderfully named imprision of a felony,
which was, simply, failing to report a felony to the
police. Since the 1967 Act, this is perfectly
reasonable behaviour and not punishable by law.*

Stormy Monday, Ruby Tuesday, Sun Comes up It's

Wednesday Morning, Friday on My Mind, Saturday Night at the Movies, Easy like Sunday Morning. Wish I could remember Thursday. Hey, that could be a song title. Wish I could forget Tuesday, more like.

So here we are, Thursday, and I still haven't managed to get to the point, but it has been a bit of a busy couple of days.

Slept like a crocodile on Tuesday night – unmoving, probably looked like a log, but at least half awake at all times, one eye open, listening to the distant sirens and the odd rumble of a heavy lorry or night bus passing the end of the road. It is never entirely quiet here, never entirely dark, and I like that, the fact that however late at night or early in the morning it might be, there is always someone else awake, some tired cleaner dragging herself to an early office job, burly maintenance men in bright orange overalls working on the underground, emergency services personnel queuing in the kebab shop, hoping for a quiet night.

But I don't usually lie awake at night listening to it all.

Glad to be single, at the moment, not that most blokes would notice any odder-than-usual behaviour, or care to mention it if they did. Yes, these are the times when it is truly a joy to have the house to yourself.

Actually I don't often have the house to myself, as I live with my best friend, Margaret, and the cat,

Cat, but they both respect my privacy. Margaret is what she would call eccentric and most people would call odd, a tall blond vague person, all hair and scarves and jangling bracelets. I have known her since we were at school and have got used to her ways and we have lived together for the last two years, sharing my house since I split up with Keith and she moved to London. She's a poetry translator, very wrapped up in her work, always wistfully in love with some married man. She's great at tea and sympathy if you ask for it, but probably wouldn't notice if I had a quiet breakdown. I often don't know if she's in or out – the only signs are bits of cotton wool on the bathroom floor, peach stones on the kitchen table, tea bags dripping on the edge of the sink, or very occasionally a miserable CD playing in the depths of her room. I've slept with one of her brothers and rung up her mother for help and advice, my brother Philip tried to teach her to drive, we had a crush on the same maths teacher when we were thirteen, we've got outrageously drunk together and gone out on the pull together more times than I can remember over the past fifteen years and we know all of each other's best stories.

Cat has lived in my house longer than I have – it was the overweight, pampered pet of the last people who lived here and they left it behind with much agonising and wringing of hands when they sold the house to me and moved to a hygienic, dust-free, double-glazed retirement flat in Surbiton, where there wasn't even a patch of concrete for their beloved cat to roll around on. I agreed to keep Cat and they knocked a grand off the house price. Bargain, I thought at the time, I'll have it put down in a week or so, or drop it off outside Battersea Dogs' Home, or give it to the Blue Cross people and nobody'll be any the wiser; but somehow it is still here, shedding fur and demanding food and purring frantically/sycophantically at the least outward sign of affection. Cat isn't allowed in my bedroom, and isn't really a worry from a secret-keeping point of view. It never listens, anyway.

Cat used to be called Fluffy, which it isn't, but has adapted without difficulty to being called Cat, Catface or Gitface, depending on whether it is in or out of favour. You have to be careful with animals' names. A friend of mine christened her new and tubby kitten Balloon, which was a cute and funny name until it got out of the house one afternoon and set off to explore the outside world and didn't come home for hours and she found herself wandering up and down the road calling out, 'Balloon, Balloon, where are you, my little Balloon?', as her neighbours wondered whether to call the police or a doctor out to have her head looked at. The creature is called Blackie now to avoid the possibility of that particular nightmare recurring.

But I digress. Another of my talents, though it wouldn't look too good on a CV. Excellent digressionary capabilities, an experienced circum-locutor, enjoys the challenge of abandoning the narrative under pressure.

Despite my comatose state on Tuesday night, I managed a couple of dreams, which would nor-mally go into the dream collection book kept under my bed but might as well go here. In the first one I was arriving back at university for another year, in a small car I knew wasn't mine, piled high with unidentified things, and I couldn't find my college, all the landmarks were out of position and the roads were cobbled, narrower than I remembered them. There were tall stone walls on either side and I knew I was almost at the right place but I couldn't see where I was and the walls were closing in or the street was narrowing and I scratched the car on a post going round a tight corner, which was going to mean trouble later, and although there were people all around, none of them seemed to hear me when I asked for help. And then when I had given up all hope of finding my college entrance, suddenly there was a gate on my right and in I went, leaving the car almost wedged in the street outside, and walked into the common room where there was an ac-commodation list without my name on it, and I saw some people that I knew but they were all people I had never liked or got on with and I realised I was going to have to ask them for help, and what if these people I had always thought were too boring or badly dressed to bother with hadn't liked me either ...?

Fortunately before I had time to find out, I was back at my parents' house, the one we lived in when I was small, and it was further out in the country than it should have been, but this was OK. I knew it was wrong but didn't mind at all. I went outside to look for my parents. I knew they were in the garden or the fields, and as I went out I heard aircraft overhead and realised that I had brought these planes somehow, they had come because of me and as they came nearer and swooped lower over the fields I knew they were bombers, they were firing at my family on the ground and the houses all around were also being hit. The noise was incredible and there was nothing I could do, the ground was being torn up by bullets and becoming muddy and I burrowed myself deep down into the mud like an animal, finding a sort of half-overgrown ditch to wriggle into, and I covered my face with it, plastering my skin in muck, my hair and clothes smothered in an attempt to hide because they couldn't just kill everyone in sight, no, I knew that they would come back in their jeeps and on foot and make quite sure there were no survivors.

As I was saying, Thursday. Suppose in the interests of continuity I should do Wednesday first. What is it they're always saying at training school? Communications must be concise, to the point, not repetitive ... oh yeah, and in the right order and consecutive is good too.

OK then, Wednesday.

Got up, washed face in very cold water to clear away the last traces of bad dreams, got dressed (wide black trousers, cream and green striped shirt, black jacket), did hair (two swipes with brush, twist at back, large silver-coloured clip), had breakfast (slice of cold vegetable pizza with extra spinach and olives from my side of the fridge, apple from communal fruit bowl, glass of mineral water from Margaret's side of the fridge), walked to the tube. Spotted Cat slipping out of a front door down the street, caught the flash of a brightly striped dressing gown as the woman inside turned to close the door; it didn't see me and set off jauntily on its own private business, tail up, pleased with its little cat life. Bought paper from cheery cockney paperman at tube entrance. Usual friendly transaction – I hold out coins, he holds out paper, we swap coins for paper. Grabbed seat on tube under nose of elderly crone – she doesn't have to go to work; if she needed a seat, she would wait until later to travel – read front page of paper, started crossword. Off tube, into building, grunt at doorman, up stairs (good for the legs) into office. First one in as usual, put on coffee (good for the brain), slump at desk, leaf through papers which have mysteriously appeared since last night. Scan room – not likely to win many design awards, curling Wanted and Missing posters on otherwise bare walls. Get up, hang yesterday's jacket on coat stand by door with other discarded items. Drink coffee, thus able to speak amicably to others as they arrive.

First is my supervisor, Julie Eliot. She's very serious, very dedicated, hardly ever sees her kids except the two weeks she takes off as annual leave every August, a scruffy, scatty, clever woman, a chain-smoking crime-busting thief-taking one woman whirlwind. Hell to work with, as she expects everyone to work the same long hours she does, but a very good person. In a just world she'd head a burglary squad or a robbery squad, something more prestigious than a juvie unit, but in this world the surprise is that she ever got promoted, rather than that she ended up with a job to do with kids. She has very short black hair, which, I think, is dyed, although I'd never ask, and a tiny figure – looks like a kid herself some days, if you don't spot the world weary eyes. (Black coffee, two sugars, in the blue and white Honeyfarm donkey sanctuary mug.)

DC Steadman, Steady, last in as usual, bulging black sports bag over his shoulder, carrying the internal mail as if to prove he's been at work for ages. He's an old style policeman, if you catch my drift. Believes the end justifies the means. Doesn't like working for a woman, and therefore spends a large proportion of his time at headquarters trying to get on to a major investigation squad of some sort. He's got a bit of a beer gut, and his round red face can't quite carry off the boyishly short haircuts he favours, but he obviously reckons he's a real ladies' man none the less. Fancies himself, even if nobody else does. Julie got a laugh the other day when he bought that black bag to replace the old grey one he used to carry. She said he must have bought the black one to try and make himself look slimmer. Now he tells everyone that's why he got it. Always has a little plastic comb sticking out of his back pocket. He's on some sort of unofficial black-list, and has been told he will not be moved any-where for the foreseeable future, apparently – something to do with an Equal Opportunities course last year, where he was heard to say that he personally never believed rape allegations made in January because they are all made (up) by married women feeling guilty after having it away at their works' Christmas party.

But he's not bad at his job. I really think his sexism and racism are all mouth, only skin deep – his victims think the world of him; they'd never believe what he says about them, though – but he just can't be bothered sometimes. A lot of his cases end up with the victim withdrawing the complaint. Less work for him, some would say, but a lot less stress for the victim in the end. (White, but strong, two sugars, in the Millwall mug – his team, al-though he hasn't been to a football match in living memory.)

Usually we're busy from the word go. We handle

a wide variety of juvenile-related cases, cover child interviews and video statements for other departments. I do the odd sexual assault statement or chaperoning job, Steady always has his nose in everyone else's business and Julie has the organisational side of things to keep her occupied. She also quietly maintains contact with some policewomen's network. I've never been asked to join, so I can only assume it's top secret and will one day emerge into daylight to depose the chief constable in a bloodless coup and replace the Jurassic-Park-load of superintendents with a new hierarchy of intelligent women. Well, I hope so.

However, today was the day the new big boss was due to arrive – our new head of department, so to speak, the last DCI having failed to turn up for work one day a couple of months ago and not having been seen since. Apparently he's sold his house, gone stark staring mad and tried to announce his belief in reincarnation to the police newspaper, inviting like-minded souls to visit him and discover their former lives. This was never published, sadly, but Steady got hold of a copy of the letter somehow – trawling through other people's in-trays, I suppose, 'basket-ratting' – and it makes frightening reading. Obviously it was circulated within hours and now everyone knows quite how mad the man was, while to all intents and purposes functioning adequately as a DCI.

Odd how quickly some people can crack up. I

remember finding a woman singing hymns in the middle of the Strand once, a hugely fat and utterly mad woman in a billowing flowery dress and little white ankle socks, no shoes, and she had a pay slip on her from the previous Friday which showed that only three days earlier she'd been working as a nurse. I asked her if I could help in any way – my favourite approach with mad people – and she took me by the hand and tried to get me to play with her in the traffic. I took her into custody at Charing Cross and she took off all her clothes and started doing aerobics. Built up quite a queue outside the cell door.

Men are pigs, especially policemen. Or do I only know policemen? Seems like it these days ... but I digress again. Seriously, though, you try and work out how to have a social life when every eligible male you ever meet is a victim, a criminal or a policeman. Who would you go out with? OK, so you do run into the odd psychiatric social worker and force medical examiner from time to time, but they tend to be very odd indeed.

So the former DCI is still officially on sick leave but his successor starts today and we're all keen to make a good impression. We've been winding up some of our longer-running cases, and farming out the not-really-our-remit ones we've taken on to help out, in preparation for today when we show the new man what an efficient and hardworking unit we are, how well we function and how much better we'd be with some extra resources.

So we were still sipping coffee and flicking through our morning papers (*Guardian*, me; *Independent*, Julie; *Sun* and *Mail*, probably lifted from someone else's office, Steady) when the door flew open and in comes Vic Nolan, the DI, top button undone, tie askew and white hair fluffed out at all angles. He doesn't mean to throw doors open any more than he means to tread on people's toes or spill food and drink wherever he goes – it seems that the complicated thought processes he maintains use up almost all the available brain cells, leaving a bare minimum free for motor functions. Well, that's my theory, anyway. Maybe he is just a clumsy old bugger.

'Anyone seen the new boy?' he asked, settling violently on Steady's desk and dislodging a file of papers that floated to the floor. 'He was due in the area commander's office at eight and there's been no sign.'

Julie seemed unconcerned. 'We were expecting him round about now,' she said. 'I do think he should have rung or something. Typical bloody man not to phone in – I mean, it's not much to ask, is it? You have been promoted and start this week, please try and make it into your office at some stage, if it isn't too much trouble, or at least make the effort to ring in and say you can't be bothered. I reckon he's got cold feet, maybe the job's too much for him and he knows it. Or maybe he's got lost.'

'Unlikely,' said Steady, stirring round the scattered papers with one toe. 'I used to be on the dip squad with him, before he went up north on promotion – he knows London like the back of his hand. More likely he's hooked up with some tart from way back and can't drag himself out of bed.'

Vic made for the door, almost kicking over the wastebin. He disappeared momentarily into the corridor, then poked his head back through the door. 'If he does turn up here, get him to ring me, will you?' he said. 'I'd like a word sometime today, if at all possible, and Lord knows what the area commander's going to say.'

Steady just sat tipped back in his chair behind his desk, ostensibly reading his paper, looking smug and knowing, and after a minute I cracked.

'Go on then – tell us all the gossip,' I said. 'I know you're dying to. What's he like to work with, why's he coming here, is he going to want to change things? Will he sign my appraisal if I ask for a couple of courses?'

Steady pursed his lips, deliberating, then decided to share some of his extensive knowledge on the subject of Fraser MacDonald, our missing leader. 'He was my DS on the old dip squad – good bloke to work for in those days. Never went home until he'd got at least one body in; we used to work well past midnight if he thought we'd get a good body out of it in the end. I remember there was this one time we was having a bundle in the middle of Oxford Street, me and him and a couple of South American dips. His was about seven feet tall, no kidding, and built like a brick shithouse; mine was nearly as tall and twice as wide and we couldn't get any assistance because it was a football Saturday and the boys were all tucked up with bodies in all over the place, and ...'

And he was off on one of his fairy tales about the good old days, when everyone knew the score and you could give someone a good kicking in the back of the van and they'd thank you for it. Julie and I were too impatient to let him get away with it this time.

'Come on, Steady,' Julie coaxed, 'we don't want to know about the glory days in the early seventies, man, we want to know what he's like now. You must have some contacts in his old area – why's he coming back here? Is he in with the chief?'

Steady looked into the depths of his empty coffee mug.

I refilled it.

'He's been under a bit of a cloud, to be honest,' he said slowly. 'I can't say how much truth there is in the rumours, but you'll hear them soon enough. There's been a bit of bother with one of the civilian staff up there, some tart typist or civvie clerk at their area headquarters, and they did say he was going to be disciplined, but then the next you hear he's been promoted out of trouble and on his way, so I guess he has got friends in high places. If you know what

I mean. Probably plays golf with the deputy, that sort of thing. But as I said, he was a good bloke in the old days. I remember the stories about him when he was in uniform – you know the one about the magistrate who found the blokes guilty and then at the end said, 'and I never want to see that knife in my court again, officer'? That was MacD in his youth. And we had some times in the old dip squad.'

I had heard the story but couldn't remember the details at all. 'What was that story again?' I asked, knowing Steady would enjoy recounting the tale.

'Well, it goes back to the days when life was a lot simpler for all of us than it is today – I'm talking pre-PACE, well before your time.'

I was lucky when I first learnt my law that the Police and Criminal Evidence Act had been in for seven or eight years, but I know some of the older officers had trouble adjusting to it.

'One time there was a lot of pressure on for figures for some reason,' he continued. 'There was some review going on forcewide and every area commander was shit scared of coming out with the worst figures or something, so we were all told we had to get at least one body in a day or we were in trouble, and, of course, with everyone out and about looking for work, it got harder and harder to get a decent job in. So some of the boys had to improvise from time to time – we all did – and one week, well MacD goes in front of the stipendiary magistrate at Bow Street with an off. weap. case, produces a flick knife, and says he was threatened with it by the old Irish drunk in the box. Drunk says he can't remember, case is proved, MacD's got his figure in for Monday. Tuesday, he's in Bow Street with a public order job, produces a flick knife, says the geezer was waving it around in a threatening manner in the Strand. Geezer denies it, calls MacD a cunt, court is shocked, case found to be proved. Wednesday, he's in Bow Street again with another off. weap. Case proved again and as he's on his way out the magistrate calls him back in, and says to him, 'I can only admire your zeal, officer, but I never want to see that knife in my court again, do you understand me?' So Thursday he draws a blank and by Friday he's at Horseferry Road court with a violent drunk with a kitchen knife ... Fucking excellent bloke he was back then – those were the days, kid.'

Well, we now knew a little about the mysterious new man, but he still didn't turn up as the morning wore on. Hot again, no air conditioning, and there was a curious tension in the office. I was being perfectly normal, not too quiet, not too chatty, hardly thinking about the previous day at all. There was a lot to be getting on with and I was going to Crown Court in the afternoon to hear the legal argument at the start of the Candy trial. Lunch time, I went up the echoing staircase to the canteen for a sandwich and, as I often do, coincidentally happened to bump into Jim Justice, usually known as JJ. Well, Justice is such a silly name for a copper, although there are worse – I've worked with a DC Crooks a few times, there's a chap in Traffic called PC Leathers who always has a hard time on Gay Pride marches and there's a Sergeant Naughtie in the Prosecutions Department.

I joined with JJ in 1991 and he's been on the major incident team for a while now. He's HOLMES-trained and gets to know everything big that's going on in the area. HOLMES is supposed to mean Home Office Large Major Enquiry System, but the HOLMES team can give you any number of alternatives. He's passed part one of his sergeant's exam but is staying in CID for the moment rather than taking part two and going back into uniform as a police sergeant. I'm almost sure he's not a mason, although he has been known to play golf.

'Hiya, JJ, what's happening in the grown-up world?' I said, joining the queue behind him at the snack counter and ignoring the protests from the rest of those awaiting their proper turn.

'Oh, loads, but it is all need-to-know stuff,' he answered. 'How are things in the kiddie league?'

'Noddy's fallen out with Big Ears, and the gollies are up in arms,' I sighed.

'You can't say "gollies",' he protested. 'Haven't you been on the Equal Ops course yet? I'm sorry but I'll have to ask you to amend your language or I will be forced to report the matter to Complaints and Discipline via the force grievance procedure.'

'Fuck off, you ugly ginger tosser.'

'OK.'

He must know he's not ugly, although he is undeniably ginger, and no offence was taken. We went over to sit by the window, taking a plate of cheese and onion sandwiches (mine), a plate of chips (mine), a seafood salad (JJ's), and two glasses of orange (work it out). JJ paid for me, making some remark about knowing how to treat a girl to a meal now and then. I pointed out he still owed me a fiver from the bet we'd had on how long it would take for the old DCI to go sick once news got about that his mad letter had been intercepted and circulated. He dug into his pocket and settled the debt with a handful of change. He has lovely hands, JJ – they always look clean, the sort of hands you can imagine touching your skin, if he wasn't such an old friend.

Police canteens always seem to be on the top floor – for many reasons. To discourage unnecessary use. To promote fitness. To reduce the chances of being caught loitering by the guv'nors, most of whom eat apart in the senior officers' room. To remind desk-bound officers of the world outside. Whatever, we have a great view over central London.

'Actually there's not much on,' JJ said. 'We've still got that arson going on, and the paedophile ring thing is exploding' – I managed not to snigger – 'and there's two new unidentified bodies on the patch, so no change there. I'm going to run away and join the Derbyshires and be a village bobby one of these days – go round on a bicycle visiting all those lonely housewives ...'

'I thought the Derbyshires failed their efficiency test or whatever they call it,' I objected.

'Exactly,' said JJ with satisfaction. 'They'll jump at the chance of getting one of London's finest.'

'Yeah, but will they want you?'

After lunch I wandered through into the Crime Desk office, a stuffy room where three fans waft the stale air round and round while papers pile up until someone activates the shredder – we're supposed to be aiming for a paper-free system, where every-thing goes straight on to computers. Some chance. And even if it did what are the chances that anyone would ever access the information, or even, maybe, analyse it? Slim to anorexic, I'd say.

Casually I trawled through the Crime Reporting Information System reports from the previous day. Mainly uninspiring stuff, purses snatched or sneaked, dodgy-looking blokes hanging about here and there, objects mislaid and never recovered. Or discovered and never claimed. Two new uni-dentified bodies, as previously mentioned by JJ. I wasn't surprised to see that the one in the alleyway had been cleaned out – no wallet, no papers, no watch, no identifying features. It is not the sort of area to leave anything just lying around – particu-larly in the evenings – even a large male body. The reporting officer had suggested a robbery gone wrong, typical victim-fights-back-and-gets-head-bashed-in sort of scenario. Hmmm. There were few details and nothing about the report suggested that the death was anything out of the ordinary for that area. I wouldn't comment, couldn't ask how it was going or contact the reporting officer for a chat. I simply did not want to know; it was none of my business. I worked with children, not dead bodies. Someone else could weep for him. I read on, preserving an appearance of calm while inwardly curling up small and refusing to accept responsibility.

The other body was a female, late twenties, battered and then burned and then dumped in the bin on the grim grey high-rise estate visible from our canteen window. Usual procedure would be to try and get a match from missing reports, then try fingerprints if obtainable, then circulate details via the *Police Gazette* to other forces and try to get a match with dental records. Some bodies stay unidentified for years, as neglected in their cold storage as they must have been in life.

Every police officer has to deal with death from time to time, whether you're a uniform officer on the beat, pushing open a shed door to find a maggoty body swinging from the roof with its trousers down, or a detective sitting in intensive care, hoping that the silent bandaged figure in the bed will recover enough to whisper a name, croak out one last message before it croaks, or whoever picks up the phone and gets lumbered with delivering a death message.

It is weird, you go to a house in order to tell the elderly couple inside that their only child has been killed, and within minutes they are apologising to you, saying how awful it must be for you to have to bear such tidings. You bring them a cup of sweetened tea, perch awkwardly on their floral chairs, try not to look at the brass-framed smiling family photographs on the polished sideboard, and they try and make polite conversation, and yet the moment you turn up on the doorstep and say, 'Are you this person? Do you have a son called that?', they know why you are there, although they may try and find an alternative explanation, any other reason at all why you might be there at half past eleven at night with such a serious look on your face. 'Oh, has he been arrested again?' they say brightly. 'Do come in, officer, I'll put the kettle on.' And you know you are in for the whole desperate life story of the seventeen-year-old runaway boy who's just died in the middle of the high street from sniffing butane, or the fifty-year-old schizophrenic who's jumped under an intercity train, after leaving home without his medication at the start of the week. You end up saying things like, 'It was all over so quickly he can't have felt a thing . . .' as if that will help, after the lifetime of pain these damaged people have had. And then there are the elderly gents who turn up face down in the river; ever tried telling an eighty-year-old woman with no other living family that her husband won't be able to push her wheelchair out to the park everyday now because he's dead?

Every time you ring someone and say, hello, I am DC Barratt ringing from whatever police station, they expect bad news. Imagine doing a job where nobody is ever pleased to see you. Everyone will tell you that it is the kids' bodies that are the hardest to deal with, and that is true by and large, although some adults seem harder than others. I had to do a death message one time to the estranged wife (hello, I'm PC Barratt, you must be the widow Jones) of a badly burned body I'd just spent a couple of hours with, waiting for Scenes of Crime Officers because initially it looked like a suspicious death, and as I stood in her kitchen telling her the news I could still smell her dead husband's cooked smell coming off my coat and I wanted to ask if she could smell it too, but managed not to. And I can still remember the smell of blood off the first fatality I went to – a man who'd been hit by a train, both legs severed. He'd been lying with his neck on one line, trying to commit suicide, when a train came along the other way and cut his legs off. Well, he managed to kill himself but not as quickly as he must have intended. If it hadn't been at night he would've been seen and rescued, because the train wheels somehow almost sealed off the amputations, but not quite, so he bled slowly for most of the night. My period had started in the car on the way down, a day early and unexpected, and I stood by the body and thought, I can smell blood, is it him or me? Has anyone else noticed?

And when I finally got home that night Keith was still up, drinking beer, smoking rollies and eating popcorn, and watching a gory horror film where people in badly lit houses were being stabbed and slashed by a huge man with a partially hidden face. He was really into the film and wasn't interested in anything I wanted to say, just didn't want to hear about my day at work. But then, he'd been really anti me joining the police in the first place, felt that I had turned and joined the enemy, and always seemed to be pleased when I had a bad day.

Background checks

NB: CHILDREN AND YOUNG PERSONS ACTS
(VARIOUS)
Basically children need looking after. Often their parents are not the best people for the job and alternatives may be considered and the wishes of the child should be taken into account in deciding this. Oh, and you can't do much with or to them without a social worker present. Suits me.

Spent the afternoon in court up to 1630 hrs, when

they stop for the day in case the judge is tired. It really angers me that the witnesses and victims and police officers have to sit around for days on end just to be sure that they are to hand to give evidence when required – so that the judge is never kept waiting. I mean, how important can one person be? This afternoon they were discussing the admissibility of some of the evidence, admissions made by the suspect to friends, things said to lawyers and overheard by police officers, statements made and then withdrawn by the suspect's girlfriend, also believed to be involved in some of the offences. All very complicated stuff, and nobody was surprised when many of the decisions made were in direct contradiction to those made at the previous hearing.

I visited Candy on my way home, met her from school and walked her back to her house, as agreed by phone with her mother. I can't bring myself to like Candy's mother – a large loud woman with masses of dyed red hair and a butterfly tattoo on her hefty upper arm – although I know she loves the girl and does her limited best for all her kids; she has five, with four different fathers, and she lives with yet another man now and is six or seven months pregnant again. The house is stacked with piles of clothes, bits of broken toys scattered across the thin carpets, there aren't enough chairs for everyone to sit down at once, the eldest girl has a one-year-old child herself, neither she nor her boyfriend has ever worked. It is a constant battleground where nobody ever gets enough attention, and quite honestly, Candy being kidnapped, raped and tortured was only one in the last year's catalogue of disasters. The family is supported by an array of social workers, home helps and nosy neighbours, and sometimes I feel like just another pair of hands sent by the state to help Candy's mother get through the day with enough energy left over to produce more scrawny, malnourished children.

As usual Candy was quiet on the walk home. Her mother is trying to get rehoused on the grounds that it is harmful for Candy to walk home from school along the route she was taking when she was picked up by the man with the promise of some sweets and a big telly round at his house. He actually wanted to take her younger friend, but the friend said, no way, weirdo. So Candy went. A child in need of attention. She's a small thin child with pale straight hair and freckles, all knees and elbows, awkward and hesitant. Her mother lets her wear make-up to school, and who am I to disapprove? I don't know what she was like before.

Once we got home and she dropped off her schoolbag, though, Candy perked up. It was still a hot afternoon, so we went for a walk in the park. I quite enjoy these little outings. I tell Candy about my love life, my university days, and she tells me about her best friend (a new one every week – some mothers don't like their children playing with

Candy, as if she's somehow contagious) or the fights she has with her older brother, usually over whether she's allowed to play with his Gameboy or not. Her brother's dad is still in touch with the family, unlike Candy's, so he gets more Christmas and birthday presents than the rest put together.

On one level I'm trying to show Candy that men and women don't always hurt each other, draw her pictures of a possible future, tell her she has a future even, but as her attention span is about thirty seconds at best, I'm not sure whether it does any good. I tell her that the bad man is in court again and that this time he will probably be sent to prison until he's so old he trips over his beard and dribbles and can't stand up straight with arthritis. Then he'll ask to be let out and they'll say no. Candy likes this idea, so I have to elaborate on it. We have him begging to be let out in a quavering old man's voice and Candy's shouting, 'NO! Go back to gaol and eat slugs!'

Then she went home to fight for her share of chip butties and cheap coke. I think they get homework set at her school but I've never seen Candy or any of the others actually do any. It is not my job to interfere.

So that was Wednesday at work.

I got home at about 1900 hrs, with a bagful of groceries and a slight headache from the heat and glare of the day. Walked down my street, spotting people through their open windows doing domestic things. It's a quiet little street; we're not overly neighbourly but we have got a neighbourhood watch scheme. Funny really, I happen to know that the two male adults in the family at number fourteen are active burglars – Mick and Geoff, friendly chaps, they invite us to their barbecues and we play softball with them and the younger kids on the green. And the last house on the left is run by an optimistic, do-gooder of a woman who fosters problem kids, their problems ranging from pyromania to psychosis, but generally they don't misbehave on their own doorstep, preferring to range further afield, where they are less likely to be recognised. I've called the local police out to noisy domestics and the occasional all-night party in the house backing on to mine, but our street is generally pretty quiet, as I said. I told our next-door neighbour, Vi, that I work with problem kids, and everyone now thinks I'm some sort of social worker. Which, I suppose, is fairly accurate really.

The house was a haven of peace, the downstairs windows open and the surrounding shady trees contributing to the atmosphere of cool. Margaret was in the living room, listening to one of her murmury guitar and soft voice Nick Drake CDs, stretched out on her back doing some sort of yoga, wearing baggy black leggings, my new trainers, an olive green leotard and a beaded Moroccan waistcoat. She was surrounded by and seemingly oblivious to a sea of typed, pencil-marked pages, dotted with half-empty glasses of water, apple cores, scissors, a bank statement, a pencil case, the remains of a sandwich. The ironing board was up, iron left on and hissing gently, the sofa cushions were piled up under the main window and it looked as if a small whirlwind had passed through. I picked my way through into the kitchen, where a thin and miserable Cat was staring hopelessly into its empty bowl.

'Good day at the office, dear?' Margaret called.

'Bloody marvellous,' I answered. 'Have you fed Cat?'

'Of course I've fed Cat and if it says different it is lying,' she said, wandering in and hanging around in the doorway.

I surveyed the disaster zone that was the kitchen sink and decided to skip food, the heat had killed my appetite, anyway. I picked up my swimming bag and told Margaret I'd see her later.

'Do twenty for me, will you?'

'Breaststroke or backstroke?'

'Ooh, breaststroke, please.'

The pool is my other fail-safe recover-from-any-thing refuge. There's something about the smell of chlorine and the hot shower after spending an hour in the cool water that makes me feel cleansed as well as clean. And I've got a fabulous swimming cap that always cheers me up – a green and purple monstrosity with flowers and frogs and butterflies on it, made of thick rubbery stuff. I've never seen one quite like it, and it often attracts admiring glances at the pool.

Swimming is great for not thinking about things, if you can just manage to get the right rhythm of movement and breathing, you can put yourself into a trance, almost. I love it. Your whole body feels smooth and streamlined and strong, there's the momentary babble of shouting kids and whistling lifeguards and tannoy messages of Junior to Reception and Don't Run in the Pool Area, before your head goes back under the water and all you can hear is the blubble-blubble-blubble of your own breath rushing out past your ears, until you surface to the noise and breathe in again, chlorine-scented air with odd pockets of aftershave or hairspray lingering on the surface. After a while all that matters is the rhythm of breathing and you find stupid lyrics running through your head, songs from primary school, 'My Aunt Jane she called me in', 'Vote vote vote for Mary Murray', or half-forgotten songs from years ago. At the same time you're counting, so that you know when it is time to turn and kick, gaining extra yards by undulating your body, and that's the best feeling of all, your body sliding effortlessly through the water – you know that this is how dolphins feel all the time, or birds. It is almost like not being a person for half an hour.

I exhausted myself at the pool and stumbled out to the changing room and showers. I like the way women of all shapes and sizes wander about in the shower area, all momentarily equal because there are no men present to judge them. A couple of sturdy blond au pairs fussing over three dark and noisy children, a couple of grannies gossiping as they tuck their hair into caps by one mirror, an anorexic-looking girl turning to check her rear view in the other mirror – mothers and lovers and students and teachers, we're all here doing something for ourselves. I'm always pleased with my body when I've been swimming, the feeling of power I have, knowing that I'm strong and that it all works. It's hard to explain but when I've been swimming I'm happy with the way I am: my body is sinewy not skinny, I feel like one of those Art Deco light supports not a scrawny bag of bones with a fat arse.

Margaret has a number of useful theories I've never heard from anyone else, many of which are very odd indeed but have a pleasing logic to them. She says that men who are fixated on large breasts are scared of your other bits, the dark and hidden and not-so-safe bits. She also says that female swimmers and runners and athletes in general tend to have small breasts, which just shows that the volume some poor women have to carry around is nothing more than excess body fat. I say, well, at least my tits point upwards. Wonder why I feel so at home in water – in my element, although obviously out of it? It surely isn't a back-to-the-womb thing, since my mother tried everything from gin and hot baths to jumping downstairs to get rid of me. She'd just left my father for the first time when she found out about me, and wasn't best pleased. She's always said that she loved me as much as the others once I was born, but there's always been a trace of half-remembered antagonism between us, a sort of mutual resentment. I never sleep curled up in a ball – I'm sure that comes from being insecure even before I had a self to worry about. (That is one of my most effective sad stories – men love it. And it is true.)

Walked slowly home through the warm dusty evening, passing the second-hand furniture shop where the owners were still sitting outside, lounging on old sofas and passing comment on the passersby, past the Greek bloke's chippy and the undertakers and the everything shop on the corner, down the narrow pavement of our street, in through the peeling green gate, brushed aside the crowding geraniums leaning out of tubs and pots, forced open front door, pushing back the collection of shoes, umbrellas and sports equipment on the stripy rug behind it. However messy and in need of redecoration my tall thin crumbling house may be, it is my refuge and sanctuary and I have loved it since I walked past one evening and saw the For Sale sign outside.

Collapsed on sofa, grateful that the cushions had been replaced and a slight tidying session had been attempted in my absence. Dumped a pile of dictionaries, thesauruses and scrawled-over sheets of paper onto the floor. Cat hopped up to pound energetically at my chest, dribble, breathe fishy breath into my face, circle several times and show me its arse, before finally tucking itself in under my chin and purring noisily, despite the warmth of the evening. It doesn't seem fair that I didn't end up with an elegant and self-contained cat that would sit at the window contemplating the mysteries of the universe and looking beautiful. Or an outdoor cat that would disappear for days at a time and catch its own food.

I could hear Margaret on the phone to Jonathan, one of her married men, a one-sided conversation which didn't seem to be going very well; I could hear her hesitant suggestions and quiet accusations and guess the rest. Finally she became more re-signed and agreed that, of course, she didn't expect to see him at the weekend; yes, she loved him, she really did love him; and then she was suddenly quiet as the phone crashed down.

When I say one of her married men, I don't mean to imply that she has several on the go at any one time – no, she's a faithful girl at heart, it just happens that all the men she falls for are unhappily married.

'He's going on fucking holiday with his fucking wife,' she announced furiously, 'and they're sharing a room. He says he specifically asked the hotel for single beds but I just don't believe it. He promised last year he wouldn't do it again, and he's promised to take me away for the weekend I can't remember how many times and we've not been once, the nearest we got was the time his mobile went on the M1 and, Oh honey, the little one's got a temperature, and he turned round and went straight home, dropped me at the tube at Swiss Cottage and I didn't see him for two weeks, even though he was supposed to be on a golf weekend with some of the ones from his work. It is unbelievable, he even seems to expect me to remember his stupid kids' birthdays and care if they're doing well at school or not. Like I really give a shit.'

I passed Cat over to her in silent sympathy. Cat sleepily registered the change, opened one round yellow eye, yawned hugely and then settled itself back into a comfortable curled-up shape and resumed napping.

'We could go away,' I suggested, 'once the trial's over. I'm due some leave, anyway. How about that place near Nice we went to in '95, the villa with the pool up all those steps from the road?'

'Yeah, and maybe I'll meet someone at the airport who's reasonable looking, solvent and single,' said Margaret without much hope. 'I don't ask much, really. Why is life so difficult?'

'Do you remember the waiter at the beach restaurant last time we were away?' I asked wistfully.

'Who could forget a bottom like his?' replied Margaret. 'I think I've got a picture of it somewhere

... sheer perfection in skintight denim cut-offs.'

Immediately distracted from her misery, Margaret began to look for the photograph album and holiday brochure from a couple of summers ago among the pile of junk paper, bills, recycled envelopes, money-off coupons and pizza shop fly-ers in her side of the sideboard. She dug out the photos from that last holiday, the two of us tanned and posing, draped around an impossibly blue pool, mellow brick villa behind us, scarlet flowers on the windowsills and palm trees in the back-ground, holding glasses of pastis and gazing out over the steep hillside dotted with villas dropping away to the Mediterranean, itself dotted with yachts and boats. Sadly the picture of Christophe's arse was missing.

We read loads of books and cooked huge meals on that holiday, and argued over whose turn it was to walk into town to post things or fetch things. We were both single that year too. It seemed unim-aginably far away in time and space. I couldn't re-member any of the things I was thinking about or feeling that year, and I hoped/wished that in a couple of years' time this week would seem as unreal.

I love Margaret but she drives me mad. She has no idea how messy she is and really seems to think she does her share of tidying up. Well, she probably does do half, but when you realise she makes ninety per cent of the mess. And then she can't wash up because of her eczema, so in theory she does the vacuuming instead, but the Hoover's been broken for months, so ... Anyway, we never argue about housework; eventually it gets done.

We agreed to try and go away for ten days at the start of September. We drank tea, we finished the crossword, I watered the wilting flowers, dusty dry lawn, parched vegetable garden and the terracotta pots crowded round the bench outside the back door while Margaret phoned her mother.

Quiet night in. I didn't tell her about the day before; she managed not to talk about her man. I went to bed at a reasonable time – I used to only be able to get to sleep by listening to the midnight news on Radio 4, dropping off slightly then half-waking to turn off the radio during the shipping forecast, but then I went out with a guy who went to sleep listening to music, so I went along with that. Then we split up and I lived with Keith, who could only get to sleep in complete silence, on one particular side of the bed, with the window open and the curtains drawn to shut out every chink of light. These days I can sleep more or less anywhere, any time, in noise or peace. I left the window slightly open, since my room is on the third floor, and the curtains are light enough to let in the early morning sun if there is any.

Wakened at 0443 by Cat scratching at the back door to be let out. Usually this annoys me, but as I was deep in a dream where I was lying on my back in a pool of some warm and thick semi-liquid, unable to move for fear of going under the surface, knowing I would drown if I moved but at the same time feeling myself slowly sinking, while on the far side of the pool I could see Keith with his back to me, talking to someone out of my sight ... I welcomed the diversion. Margaret never lets Cat out; she probably wakes up but knows I'll get up eventually. I suppose we could fit a cat door, but it would get ideas above its station. It's important to make it realise it needs us sometimes.

Lay awake until it was time to get up, knowing that things were not going to get any easier, that I'm going to have to think things through and decide what to do. But not just yet, please, not yet.

Review available information

NB: MENTAL HEALTH ACT 1980, SECTION 136
*Consider: police officers are held to be experts in
madness and can take anyone into custody to get
their heads checked if they think it necessary.
Actually, the only two occasions when your
opinion is useful evidence are when you say, 'I
thought he was mad' and 'I thought he was drunk'.
You do see a lot of care-in-the-community patients
wandering about these days. I have actually seen a
man on his knees barking like a dog outside a coffee*

shop. Looked a bit like one of Margaret's yoga positions.

Thursday, oh blessed relief, was a cloudy overcast day and I put on a long skirt and my big black Tank Girl boots to celebrate the cooler weather. I got into work in a reasonably good mood. Up stairs stamping powerful feet, enjoying the noise I made, kicked door open, strode into office, coffee on. There was a note on the smeary whiteboard in shaky capital letters, written in orange pen – the only colour that the boys next door haven't swiped yet – for DCI MacDonald, timed and dated yesterday at 1800 hrs: F. MACD. PHONE ME IMMEDIATELY. It was signed 'Ted Doddy', our area commander, and the signature trailed away uncertainly towards the bottom of the board, as if the author had forgotten what he had started to write, or felt the word 'immediately' was a bit too strong, or was unsure of how to spell his name.

Obviously the new DCI chap hadn't turned up late or called in sick yet. Very unprofessional.

Steady got in soon after me, unshaven, crumpled and brimming with news. 'Some of them think he's been paying some calls, settling old scores,' he announced, 'and they're ringing round the hospitals this morning in case he's been hit by a bus ... which is how I feel this morning. I haven't just got a headache, my joints ache. Maybe I'm coming down with something. Or maybe it was the Guinness. You should have come to the piss-up last night, it was a really excellent do. I was supposed to go home last night, so I'll be in trouble with the missus, but, anyway, it was worth it. DS Lampton nearly got arrested at the first pub. You know what he's like when he's had a few and some bloke banged into him on the way past to the bog, jogged his elbow and spilled his pint and that was it, handbags at ten paces, and then when we finally got out of there Monty started a fight at the second – one minute he was arguing with this bloke about whether Status Quo were better than Bowie, next thing they were trying to pull each other's heads off. Don't know who won. I saw your mate Nina from Custody with her new boyfriend. Don't know how she gets in and out of that skirt she was nearly wearing, maybe she just keeps it on? And, of course, since we didn't know the new man, I had to ask her what rank he was – told her she's been going through the ranks so fast she must be due for a chief super soon. Turns out this one's not job, he's a banker or something, so she wasn't too happy with me, but he laughed it off. Must be doing all right at his bank or whatever because he seems to be loaded – he was flashing it around in the Firkin pub, anyway –'

Then he broke off as Julie came hurrying in, changed the subject and repeated his main bit of news.

Julie looked hassled, fidgeting with the buttons on her floppy shirt, first tucking it into her narrow trousers, then draping it outside. 'I really wanted to see him today,' she said. 'There are some decisions I haven't got the authority to take myself that really can't be put off any longer. If he's not here by eleven, I'll have to go to the superintendent. A right bloody nuisance this man's turning out to be, and he hasn't even made it through the door yet.'

'What's he look like, this MacDonald bloke?' I asked.

Steady looked at me and raised an eyebrow, pausing in his administration of Resolve and vitamin C tablets from the unzipped side pocket of his capacious bag. 'Too old for you, Lou,' he replied, 'if that's what you want to know. And I don't think you're his type. No offence, but he goes for the more comfortably built ones.'

'Yeah and he likes girls who can type and do shorthand and go out with policemen, so no luck there, either,' I answered. 'I just wondered what he looked like. I mean, he could have been in the building yesterday and I wouldn't know if I'd seen him. I mean, I can usually spot a cop at thirty paces – you know, you just look for a beer-gut-and-tache combination for the blokes and sensible shoes for the women – but I don't know the distinguishing features that say DCI.'

'You can usually bet on a pair of bollocks,' said Julie helpfully, 'and they're generally –'

'Well, it has been a few years,' interrupted Steady, who doesn't like it when Julie and I set off on a we-hate-men conversation – he says we make him feel nervous and he can get that at home and doesn't need it at work too, 'but he's a bit of a ladies' man. Big chap, used to be a sharp dresser, always wore a suit, black hair, used to play rugby. As a matter of fact we were on a team together that went up to play the South Yorkshires once, quite a while ago this was, and we had to get the train back because the minibus broke down, or we were all too pissed to drive it, or the Yorkshires nicked the keys, I can't remember why it was, but, anyway, we ended up getting on this train and who should be running the buffet but this geezer I'd nicked the previous year for false accounting. Well, you should have seen his face, but he cottoned on pretty quick and that was it from then on, the free beers never stopped all the way back to London ...'

And I'd stopped listening by then because I was having one of those revelatory moments when you suddenly begin to understand something, and it takes absolutely all of your concentration to keep your discovery to yourself.

I realised that Julie was talking and made an effort to focus on the room I was in, bring myself back up to date, tune in and maybe join in. Get a grip, this could be important.

'... and I rang one of my friends who used to work in the control room at headquarters,' she was saying, 'when there was all that fuss about him. Apparently there would have been a big criminal investigation but the girl suddenly withdrew her allegation and emigrated to New Zealand. One wonders where she got the money from all of a sudden. Story is that he gave her a couple of grand to drop the whole thing and paid for her and her husband to leave the country. Still, I guess that's a better way to deal with that sort of thing than waiting a year and being quizzed about it in court. Can't say I'm looking forward to working with the man, though. If he ever turns up.'

'Maybe the girl invested some of her pay off in a hit man?' Steady suggested.

I couldn't manage to join in. 'I'm off to get a cold drink. Anyone want a coke?' I said, hardly squeaking at all.

When I got back, the office was empty and there was a new note on the board: LOU – MEETING IN LECTURE ROOM 4TH FLOOR, ASAP Jules.

Hurried along the corridor, shoved my way through the heavy swing doors – good for upper body strength, wonder if that's why they never get oiled – left into the stairwell, up to the next floor, through the next set of heavy swing doors, paused outside the lecture room to peer in. Large number of people inside – I saw Julie and Steady near the back on the right and slipped in to join them. A few faces turned to see who was arriving late, but most of the people there remained focused and attentive.

The meeting had been called by Ted Doddy, which was odd, and everyone was looking serious and concerned, which was even odder.

The area commander didn't deign to notice me – or was tactfully ignoring my late arrival. I suspect option one. He's a tall and imposing figure of a man, and he certainly looks the part with his swept-back silver hair and bushy eyebrows, but he isn't often let out in public any more and there are any number of Ted Doddy stories doing the rounds which suggest that his useful days are over. He's just waiting for the right pay off deal to take him even more comfortably into retirement.

He'd obviously just started speaking and I sat down on one of the unsteady plastic chairs.

'. . . will already be aware that our colleague Fraser MacDonald, many of you will have known him over the years, personally or by reputation' – and here he paused momentarily as if expecting assent or comment, neither of which was forthcoming – 'did not arrive as expected yesterday. The murder squad have today identified a body found on our patch late Tuesday night as that of DCI MacDonald.'

Again he paused, and this time the room erupted in shocked outbursts, everyone there wanting to know more, or express their reaction in some way. The area commander allowed a minute of confused babble before inviting DI Nolan to take over.

The DI leapt to his feet, pushing back his chair and moving into space to pace up and down as he spoke. His hair was as wild as usual and he looked as if he'd been interrupted in mid-shave. The officers in the front row tucked their feet under their chairs out of harm's way. 'OK, well, as you are all no doubt aware, Fraser MacDonald was expected to take over as head of the Sexual Offences and Juvenile units this week. His body was discovered in the alley behind the Oceana Fish Bar by the owner putting out rubbish bags in the early hours of Wednesday morning' – he looked briefly at a crumpled piece of paper from one of his jacket pockets – 'a Mr Samson, who dialled three nines. The scene was attended initially by uniform officers who called out SOCO and the duty CID man. I've made up copies of their reports to distribute at the end of this briefing. There will be sets of pictures from the scene available later on today, and I've got someone in Personnel fishing out his last warrant card picture to be enlarged and distributed for the house-to-house enquiries. Basically, he suffered extensive blunt-instrument head injuries, some wounds to the torso, believed to have been caused by broken glass, and all his property was removed from his pockets, thus causing the unfortunate delay in identification. An attempt had also been made to conceal the body under a pile of rubbish. I wanted everyone to be informed as soon as possible, but I don't propose to involve the Sex Offence or Juvenile officers in the investigation at this stage, for various reasons, so if they would like to return to their normal duties, I will now brief the rest of you as to your duties in this investigation.'

Nobody seemed in a hurry to leave – I think everyone was stunned at the news. I certainly was. I couldn't think of anything to say. The usual joky response to any such briefing was absent all round. There is always a greater sense of involvement when the murder victim is a police officer – it is as if the distancing process you usually rely on can't function properly. It is just closer to you. Everyone hates cop-killers.

However, DI Nolan clearly wasn't going to continue until he had cut down the numbers, so those of us no longer required left the room, albeit reluctantly, dragging our heels in the hope of hearing a few more details. By unspoken agreement we headed straight for the canteen to discuss the morning's news. I dropped out halfway there, swung left into the ladies' toilet, calling out, 'catch you in a minute, get me a tea, will you?' knowing I would be accused of trying to avoid the twenty-pence price of a cuppa but needing to compose myself.

Splashed some cold water on my face, struggled to get my breathing slow and calm. Old yoga trick: you pretend you are smoking, breathe in slowly, hold it, exhale in a controlled rush. Couldn't spend too long in there or Steady would have felt the need to comment on the state of my bowels. I looked at myself in the mirror, tried a smile, attempted a wink, settled for a more characteristic scowl. I looked about the same as usual, neither remarkable nor bland. My stomach was twisting in knots but that is a familiar feeling – I get like that whenever I have to give evidence in court, even when I'm going to be telling the truth ... Time to find out what was happening in the canteen.

The canteen was busy, most of the tables either occupied or cluttered with used cutlery, plates, drinks cartons and cans, yogurt pots and banana skins, puddled with cold tea and coffee. A large group of uniform officers were noisily tucking into their '999' breakfasts after a hard morning's work flat-footing it round King's Cross. A few traffic wardens were huddled in a corner, always unsure of their welcome (and rightly so, in my view), and a small gathering of civilian staff had taken over some of the window tables, nibbling at dry toast and fruit. Most of our civvies are young single women; they are always on diets and it is due to their influence that our canteen provides a range of low-cal drinks and snacks. Revolting stuff. The salads they sell would choke a donkey.

I found them assembled at the big table by the window and took my seat between Julie and Steady. Tea and a sticky bun awaited my attention. The gossip was already flying and I didn't want to miss any more of it.

Julie, Steady and I represent the entire staff of the Child Protection Unit, although when we're really busy there are other trained officers we can call in. The Sex Unit, or Sexual Offences Team as they style themselves, is a larger group with a bigger office and more resources – an altogether more prestigous place to work. There were five or six of them present today – DS Lampton, their leader, the legendary hard-drinking bald dwarf, and a selection of his finest officers.

He isn't really a dwarf, of course – although the height restriction for police officers had to be dropped to encourage more Chinese and Asian applicants, there is still the assumption that you have to look the part, and a really tiny police officer would struggle with things like public order and riot training and so on. Let me just say that he is one of the few men I know who doesn't physically intimidate me. Scary though he is in his own way.

I don't have much to do with the Sex boys and girls as a general rule, except in so far as our jobs overlap from time to time and we sometimes go to the same social functions. They all dress alike – all bleached hair and gold jewellery and too much make-up. And that's just the men.

DS Lampton was talking. 'I never met the man myself,' he said, 'but I do know that there was some merriment when the word got round that he was heading for the Sexual Offences Unit – seemed as if everyone but me was in on the joke. Anyone here know why it is so hilarious?'

Julie answered him slowly, as if reluctant to slag off the dead, speaking quietly as if trying to keep it to our table. 'Well apparently it seems that he's known as a bit of an expert in the sexual offences area. There's a story I've heard from a generally reliable source about a civilian from Eight Area Headquarters being assaulted at the Christmas do the year before last. Word is that he raped her,' she said, 'but it was never officially investigated because the girl left the country.'

Steady took up the story, dropping his voice mysteriously so the nearest Sex girl leant towards him to hear better, coincidentally exposing a large amount of cleavage. 'I used to work with him,' he said, 'and he was a good bloke in those days, but I've heard that story too, and a couple of others as well. There are a few women in the job who refuse to work with him at all now, and his own marriage was rocky when I knew him. They ended up practically separated and he has a flat in town now. And there's a twenty-year-old girlfriend somewhere around too. Apparently the CSA are on his trail ... if he wasn't Grand Master of the chief's lodge, I don't think he'd be in the job.'

'You're not serious?' I asked. 'How do you know that?'

Steady tapped his nose knowingly but said no more.

Trying to behave normally, I forced myself to join in and cast around for a sensible comment. I asked Steady if he had been serious earlier when he'd suggested that there might have been a hit man involved in Mr MacDonald's failure to appear at work.

It was Julie who answered, still sounding distracted and worried. 'Oh Lou, don't be silly, that was just a joke, we didn't even know he was dead then. And surely most professional hit men can afford a decent weapon these days. I've certainly never heard of a contract killing by bottle and half-brick, have you?'

Steady agreed, as his dunked chocolate biscuit disintegrated messily into his coffee. 'No, it doesn't look like a professional job at all. I've read the CRIS report, although I didn't pay much attention at the time, but as far as I recall, the officers on scene thought it was probably a robbery that escalated. I mean, he was a cop, he would have fought back, tried to give as good as he got – after all, we're trained to do that.'

One of the Sex girls disagreed. 'Ooh no,' she said. 'If anyone tried to mug me, I'd just give them my bag. It's not worth it these days, those kids all carry knives and aren't afraid to use them and I'd rather lose my money than my looks.'

Steady sniggered and I felt almost fond of him.

'D'you remember the self-defence lessons at training school?' I asked. 'With that little Welsh bloke who really fancied himself? They were completely useless, those lessons. I mean, how are you supposed to remember those complicated moves years later when you actually might need them? You always end up doing something instinctive, like grabbing them by the throat or something and end up being disciplined for using a non-Home-Office-approved restraint technique. Even in training it was stupid – the trainer got me in a head lock one day and I had to bite his thigh to get him to let go, and I stopped going to the classes after that.'

'Well you passed it, anyway, didn't you?' said Julie. 'Though to be honest, I'd hate to have to rely on you as my back-up in a fight.'

I didn't argue the point, although this struck me as unfair. Especially coming from someone who claimed to be five feet one and three quarters. I've always worked on the principle that if you don't look like a threat, people won't feel the need to hit you, and in general I'd rather be underestimated than have people expect too much from me. I used to trail hopelessly round the hockey pitch at school, dragging my heavy hockey stick behind me, so I never got booked for the vicious tackles I'd throw in when necessary, as they were always assumed to be mistakes.

However, it didn't seem to be the moment to point out that I'm much stronger than I look. JJ is probably the only one at work who knows that – he was on my intake and did self-defence and played football with me. I've actually been in a fight with some pissed-up football fans with him when we were in uniform, where I think I more than carried my share. Funnily enough, nobody ever complained about being smacked by me, even though I had my baton out and was swinging away for ages. I suppose being knocked on the head by a woman isn't very street cred or something.

DS Lampton got back to the point. 'Do they know when it happened?' he asked. 'It's an odd place to find a DCI in the middle of the night, given he hadn't started work here yet.'

'He went out that lunch time,' answered Steady. 'I spoke to his girlfriend, on Wednesday. She said she thought he was going to have a prowl round, get to know the patch. Looks like he had a nose for the trouble spots all right.'

I hadn't thought about another woman. Somehow it hadn't occurred to me that this man could have been loved by someone. Perhaps she'd been putting up with him for the sake of his DCI's wage packet. Maybe he'd been beating her; maybe she was secretly relieved when he never came home.

I spotted JJ loitering near the tea urn, looking bright and cheerful as usual and chatting up the grumpy woman who was actually smiling for once, falling for his charm. Don't know how he manages it. Bastard. Must be something to do with the freckles.

'What's the news?' I shouted over to him. 'Or can't you tell me?'

JJ was bound to be involved in the investigation – he always got in on the really interesting jobs. He smiled and came over to sit at the window table with us, draping his suit jacket over the back of his chair and smoothing out the wrinkles before sitting down. 'I suppose you all want to know,' he said. 'Well, I'm not quite sure what's going on, to be honest. Vic Nolan had got round to giving us all the background info and was just about to send some of the footmen out on enquiries when a message came in from the chief's secretary and the briefing was abandoned. Everyone was called back, immediate enquiries cancelled and we're supposed to be meeting again at three ... and that's absolutely all I know. Although if you get me another tea I could try and remember some more of the details for you.'

He didn't really want to chat much. Neither did I. For a man with such an open and honest face he can be very hard to read sometimes. I got the impression that I'd annoyed him. Or else, that there was something he just wasn't telling me.

Consider secondary sources

NB: WAYS AND MEANS ACT 1902

As amended by various later Acts ... Basically if you need to arrest someone or search someone or even just feel like bullying someone for a while, the law can generally be stretched or bent to cover what you're doing – they don't teach you this at training school, it is one of the first things you learn on the job – anything can be justified, if you simply begin your approach from the right angle, generally an oblique one. Police officer's philosophy.

I couldn't seem to settle down to anything. Tense nervous headache? You bet. On edge, but just about holding my balance. Keeping myself occupied, I rang the Crown Prosecution Service at court to find out how the Candy trial was progressing. Still at the legal arguments stage, apparently. I read a few pages from the small pile in my in-tray, decided that I couldn't be bothered, started to read the daily intelligence logs and gave up on those too. All those hopeful descriptions of suspects – 'male, mixed race, fairly light skin, some stubble, red baseball cap, black puffa jacket, gold upper front tooth, believed aged 15 to 16' ... 'female, bleached blond hair, aged 30–35, large build, 5ft 6in, mini skirt, smokes, pierced ears' ... 'last seen entering underground station in possession of knife with wooden handle, 5 in silver-coloured blade' ... 'white male aged 60s, grey hair, blue overcoat, brown trousers, approaches young boys, believed to offer use of his car' – and so on for several pages. Oh, very occasionally you read one and think, yes, that sounds like so-and-so, and you ring the Local Intelligence Officer and pass the information on, but more often than not the description fits so many people you can't say for sure. There aren't that many one-legged robbers or albino prostitutes or seventy-year-old con artists who lisp and walk funny.

I was in the sort of mood where I'd normally go out and walk round, checking up on my local contacts. Bearing in mind what happened last time,

I decided to give it a miss. Trouble was, when I wasn't busy I had to try harder to focus my mind on trivia, keep it ticking over with nothing in particular to keep off the one particular subject that everyone else at work wanted to discuss.

We talk a lot in our office. Steady likes to keep us up to date with the progress of his various affairs, so we know what to say to his wife if she phones. Julie talks about work, mostly – she is endlessly interested in why people do what they do, why they end up the way they do, whether there could have been other outcomes, and if so, how. She's interested in theories of justice, blame and responsibility, which is unusual in a police officer. I like to keep my opinions to myself but will happily argue about anything, so long as it's understood that I don't necessarily mean what I say.

I tried a few old favourite arguments on Steady in the canteen once. There's a great myth surrounding what the policy-makers and planners at headquarters like to call 'canteen culture', claiming that the innocent police recruits who join the job full of love for their fellow men and women learn to discriminate and hate through listening to the talk of older and more experienced officers at the canteen tables. It is true that until I joined the job I didn't know that all Scousers were car thieves, but I was told that at training school by a sergeant originally from the North Wales police. Anyway, this discussion with Steady was fairly typical of the nonsense we produce in the canteen, where we try to avoid talking about work at all, where possible.

He'd asked me what was the point of studying an obscure subject like philosophy when you could learn something useful, like how to fix your car, or computing, or engineering, like his boy was doing at college. Having considered the arguments for upwards of five seconds, he said that:

1 it is better to be a happy pig than an unhappy philosopher, because it is.
2 if you gradually replace all the timber in a boat, it doesn't matter if it is the same boat, it is still yours. You can still sail it or sell it, so who gives a toss?
3 you can't split your brain into two working halves, so why worry about which would be you if you could?
4 if hanging someone makes the general public respect the law, then it doesn't matter who you hang so long as the public believe it was a sinner.

I wish I had his certainty sometimes. I have a bit of a problem with right and wrong from time to time.

I find the subjects of justice, crime and punishment fascinating from an academic point of view and I do my best to work within the law and in the public interest, but it isn't always clear if the current system really works. Or if it is really meant to. Of course, we all want justice: from the tiny child crying 'but that's not fair' to the little old dear determined to have her day in the small claims court, it is what we demand. If we only knew what it was.

As a police officer, you might think I should have acted and reacted differently these past few days. All I can say is, I've seen the random nature of great British justice. I defy anyone to spend a single afternoon at a magistrates' court and emerge with their faith in the system intact. Or look at crown courts, where a case can go through the argument stage, a jury will come in, and then the case will fail for whatever reason. The next time it is heard the arguments are presented again and a totally different interpretation of the guidelines will result in the second jury being asked to consider a completely different selection of the available evidence.

All day the conversation kept coming back to the dead DCI and eventually I went into the empty office at the end of the corridor to make a couple of phone calls in peace and hopefully privacy, although you can never be sure in a police station. I rang my mother. No answer. Would have maybe rung my father if I'd known his new number. My mother probably had it, but even if she had been in, I would have felt odd asking her for it. I rang home and listened to our ansaphone message telling me we were 'unable to reach the phone at that moment due to it being on a very high shelf'. Made a mental note to change it some day soon. Left a message for Margaret, suggesting we meet in town this evening for a few beers or a chilli or something.

I looked out of the window at the little people below, scurrying about their various little businesses, never looking up at the sky or even taking their eyes off the pavement. Something you have to learn quickly when you come to live in the city – look up at the sky, follow the flight of a pigeon or watch the top branches of a tree in the wind and you'll either slide in dog shit, trip on a paving stone, catch the eye of a bully or madman, or be mown down by a bike courier.

Eventually I got bored with looking down on people. I went back to my desk and happened to pass the door to the murder squad incident room on the way – well, it's nearly on the way – and found it to be locked. Most unusual. There were raised voices inside but I really didn't want to be seen with my ear stuck to the door.

Without really thinking about it, I have quite clearly decided that I'm going to keep what happened on Tuesday to myself. Well, it is getting a bit too late to tell anyone. Try and remember any other time I've managed to keep a secret for any great length of time. Fail. Remember that I never told anyone at college when Kara had an abortion. Well, not for years. Feel slightly more hopeful.

So I joined Julie and Steady in the general isn't-it-awful? what-can-have-happened? have-you-heard-the-latest? discussion. Since we weren't going to be involved in the official investigation and were therefore not privy to all the known facts, we were free to improvise, invent and generally speculate. The phone kept ringing, interrupting us with conversations like this:

'Hello, Child Protection Unit, DC Barratt speaking.'

'Oh hi, Louisa, it's Nina here, how's it going?'

'Fine thanks. How are you?'

'Not too bad. Same old crowd down here. Hey, what is this I hear about a body being ID'd as your new DCI? Sounds too weird to be true.'

'Oh, it's true all right.'

'Had he started yet? Did you know him at all? What was he like? The gossip's going crazy – someone was saying he had his head smashed in, so they had to ID him from dentals, is that right?'

'You'd have to ask someone in the incident room, Nina, we're not exactly in on this one.'

'Did you hear about the rumour from Eight Area, about him being a bit of a sleazebag? Doesn't sound right somehow, poor guy's lying in the mortuary or wherever, but apparently he's been that close to being busted back to uniform on a number of occasions, and one of the gaolers here knew him as a DS and he reckons he was well into all sorts of dodgy business even then – God, I can't remember anything like this. Have the press got hold of it yet?'

'Seriously, I don't know much about him. As I say, you'd have to talk to someone on the team.'

'Yeah, well maybe I will. Hey, are you going to the robbery squad do on Friday?'

'Haven't decided yet. I suppose I probably will. What about you? Are you on speaking terms with them after they lumbered you with those four kids in for ID parades the other week?'

'Yes, that was a bit off, wasn't it? I think I made my feelings felt. But that DS Andrews is a real sweetie though, isn't he? But so intense. I'll probably see you there then. I'm on earlies, so I should make it ... Oh, listen to this one – did you hear about the strange case of the missing meals? Well you see, someone got bored and did an audit and discovered that there's about fifty prisoner's meals – you know, those awful microwaveable chicken madras things – gone missing from the storage room in the back of Custody and the inspector's only gone and searched everyone's lockers for them, even mine. I mean, I have underwear in there and everything, and as I said, as a vegetarian, you'd think I'd be above suspicion. Of course, they never found the meals, but I hear some interesting items were discovered, bits and pieces that had found their way out of the old property store ... Anyway, can't say too much while it is all going on but there'll be a couple of people getting Reg. 7s before the week is out. Still, you've got to give the

Complaints and Discipline people something to keep them busy, stop them from snooping around too much. Say hi to Julie for me, and tell that arsehole Steadman he owes me at least an apology and probably a grovel for the other night! Bye!'

Locker searches happen every now and then, it is a fact of life, the top brass like to keep everyone on their toes. They swoop on CID offices from time to time too, supposedly at random, going through officers' drawers. Dread to think what they might find in here, Steady's none too careful to put it mildly. Imagine if they searched houses too. Start to think about that idea, realise it is unlikely to happen, but what if they had reasonable suspicion? Christ, even my computer paper is nicked from here. I've got a load of old interview tapes in the loft that should have been destroyed years ago ...

'Hello, Child Protection Unit, DC Barratt speaking.'

'Oh, good afternoon, this is DI Gregory, London South Crime Squad ... I'm not sure if you can help me, I was supposed to meet DCI MacDonald next week and I see on the message system that he's been murdered. Is this some kind of a joke or what? I spoke to him on the phone last week, he sounded OK then and gave me this number to get in touch.'

'Well, he was due to work here but we never got to meet him. Unfortunately it does seem to be true, his body has been formally identified.'

'Jesus, what happened?'

'You'd have to talk to the incident room, we've not been involved. I can tell you he was found on our patch in the early hours of Wednesday, in an alleyway used by the local toms – head injuries and cuts, pockets emptied, but that's about all I can say. I don't think the press have been told yet.'

'Well, thanks, I'll keep it quiet at this end then. Come to think of it, they'll probably try and keep the whole thing hushed up for a while – doesn't look good, does it? I bet they don't tell the press anything, at least until they know what he was doing there. I'll just give the incident team a ring, see if we can help at all.'

Finally a phone call I could manage almost effortlessly.

'Hello, Child Protection Unit, DC Barratt speaking.'

'Hiya, matey. Margaret here.'

'Go ahead, over.'

'Is that your best telephone voice? That's not going to impress anyone, you should make more of an effort. What was I ringing you for? Oh yeah, what time are you finishing? I'm in town until about six thirty, although I could hang around if need be. Shall I call for you or wait for you or what?'

'Oh, I can finish round then. Meet me in the Stag?'

'OK, I could do with a drink, it has been one of those days.'

'You've had one of those days? Wait till you hear about mine ... See you later.'

'Bye.'

Strange sort of afternoon, really – couldn't concentrate on work, kept nipping out for snacks. I haven't stopped eating today, must be down to nerves or something, also I kept hoping I'd bump into someone off the investigative team to find out how they were progressing. I finally ran into JJ on my way out. I was heading down the front steps as he was climbing them, two at a time as usual, not even out of breath. We met halfway.

'Haven't seen you look so cheerful for days,' he said. 'Could it be you're going home?'

'No, better than that, I'm going to the pub,' I replied. 'I'm meeting my housemate in the Stag. D'you fancy a drink when you finish?'

'Could be a while yet,' he said. 'There's still a few things that need doing today but I'll pop in on my way past if I get out before closing time, see if you're still there.'

I wanted to ask what was going on, what the current theory was, what forensics they had, whether any witnesses had come forward. Whether they had any suspects. I managed a smile instead. 'Maybe see you later then,' I said. 'Don't work too hard.'

Communication skills

NB: CRIMINAL LAW ACT 1967, SECTION 5 (1)
Describes the offence known as compounding an arrestable offence – this is where you know or believe that an arrestable offence has been committed and you keep quiet about it in return for some consideration. You can get two years' imprisonment for this, but you'd have to be very unlucky to get caught ...

Margaret was already in the pub when I got there,

sitting at a large table which she'd managed to keep free from other drinkers despite the crowd. Probably something to do with the peculiar faces she pulls when deep in thought. I've never seen the need to tell her about that particular habit. She was finishing off the *Telegraph* crossword, muttering under her breath, 'Dangly bits, nine letters, genitalia?'

She'd got me a large gin, always a pleasant sight after a long day at work, but I was so thirsty I went to the bar for a coke to drink first. I got served fairly quickly, which is unusual for me – I'm usually too polite to have much of a bar presence. Well, I was brought up not to push myself forward, not to make a fuss, always to consider other people before myself. I've spent the last ten years trying to adjust to the rest of society but it isn't always easy.

Margaret is better at it than me – she's not exactly pushy, but she will say if she thinks it's her turn. Even when it isn't.

'So tell me about your day before I bore you with mine,' she said, as I sat down facing her.

'Oh, God, Margaret, you wouldn't believe what's happened at work,' I began.

'Um, let's see, they've chosen a woman as the new chief constable, the canteen had something edible on for lunch, they've increased your budget, you've fallen in love with that Steady bloke, he's fallen for you too, you've got a commendation, a medal, you've had another complaint, you got your

P45 in the post, that trial's collapsed again, am I getting warm yet?'

I laughed. 'No, nowhere close.'

'OK, let me think. You've been given a driving course, Julie's run off with the cleaner, they're putting you back in uniform to do traffic?'

'Margaret, our new boss has turned up.'

'So what's the big deal?'

'He's turned up dead in an alleyway and I can't find out what's going on.'

Margaret appeared suitably gobsmacked, holding up both hands and staring at me wide-eyed in mock horror. 'What do you mean?'

'Well, I really need to know what's being done, how the investigation is going ...' I began to improvise, seeing a way to get it off my chest. You can tell Margaret anything, she never really listens. 'Look, this is top secret, OK, not a word to anyone, but one of the girls who works on Eversholt Street might know something about him, but she's scared to come forward and I don't know if it's important or not. Anyway, I've asked JJ to come along later so I can find out a bit more, he's collating all the info in the incident room.'

'That's not been on the news,' Margaret said. 'I had the radio on all afternoon. Hasn't the body been identified or what?'

'I don't know why it's being hushed up, maybe JJ'll know. So that's my news – how was your day?'

Margaret swirled the remnants of ice cubes round

in the bottom of her glass. 'Bloody awful, actually,' she stated reflectively. 'I rang Jonathan at home and his wife answered, said he was at work. I thought, funny, he was supposed to be taking a day's leave, so I rang him at work. Seems he told them he had to take the day off because his wife's sick. So I rang him again at work and pretended to be his wife . . . I was really cross at him, I thought he was two-timing both of us. Then he rang me at home. Turns out he'd taken the day off to make up a picnic and was on his way round to take me out on a river boat down to Richmond Park. So I said I had too much work on and he said if I was too busy to see him, he wouldn't trouble me again. So that's that, and when he finds out about my phone calls he'll be ever so angry.' She drank the last of her gin. 'So I went shopping to cheer myself up!' and she produced a small bag from under the table. 'What d'ya think?' she said, holding up a small shiny turquoise top. 'My colour or what?'

A man in a suit standing nearby leaned over towards her. 'Why don't you try it on here?' he suggested. 'I'll tell you if you look better with it on or off.' His friends, a group of similar men-in-suits, raised their glasses and laughed appreciatively.

Margaret smiled sweetly and fluffed out her hair. 'Buy me a drink?' she suggested, in her best dumb blond style, 'and maybe I will.'

The man nearly dropped his pint in shock. He went to the bar and brought back a pair of fresh drinks in no time.

'Thanks,' said Margaret, placing one in front of me and sipping from the other. Then she turned her back on him and carried on talking to me. 'About this holiday we're having,' she said. 'Can we make it any earlier?'

The man-in-suit was obviously trying to work out where he'd gone wrong. His friends had started to laugh at him now and he was beginning to look annoyed. I had one eye on the door and was patting my back pocket – you wouldn't find me in a tricky situation again without my warrant card, although I wouldn't want to get it out except in an emergency. Mind you, the chances of me and Margaret getting arrested for being in a pub fight are pretty slim, given that the average policeman or woman would assume we were innocent bystanders and we'd be able to slip away – probably crying – before anyone found out quite how much damage we'd done. (Margaret knocked someone out in a college bar once.)

Anyway, I was glad to see JJ pause on the pavement outside and squint in. I waved him over and the man-in-suit decided not to bother. JJ's on the large side, and you can tell from a distance that it is mainly muscle not fat, although he's not one of those thick-necked, muscly blokes that spend all their spare time flexing in front of mirrors.

I introduced JJ to Margaret, thinking as I did so that JJ would assume I was matchmaking. Margaret would know better, I hoped – we leave each other's love lives alone, since we rarely approve of each other's choices. Actually, it might just work – although JJ's single, he's a couple of years older than Margaret, he's better looking than most coppers, and he's got a brain – how come I didn't think of this earlier? Poor chap can't help being ginger, after all, and at least he does his best to distract attention from his hair by always dressing with impeccable style. He's the only policeman I know who was actually upset when Versace got shot.

Since Margaret is so fair and I'm on the dark side, both in hair and complexion, we don't often have man problems because my men don't tend to fancy her and vice versa. Which is important in a girly friendship, I find. Wish I could say the same about me and my sister Josie – my boyfriends always used to fall for her and in the end it got ridiculous, she could only ever come round when they were out and in the end we kind of stopped bothering.

JJ went to the bar and returned with an armful of crisps and snacks. 'Health food,' he explained. 'Potatoes, for vitamin C, spring onions, cream cheese and more veggies – chives.'

Margaret ripped open a couple of packets of crisps and mixed a large handful, adding a couple of dry roasted peanuts to the mixture. 'Lovely,' she pronounced, repeating the process. 'Cheers,' she added, raising her glass. 'Here's to us and those that like us – damn few and getting fewer.'

JJ looked amused. 'That's a good toast,' he said. 'I must remember it for the next time we solve something – I don't know if Lou's told you, but I work in the major incident room and we traditionally celebrate large at the end of our investigations. Especially if we actually get a result.'

Margaret opened her eyes wide and looked fascinated. 'That sounds awfully important,' she said. 'You must be very good to get into that sort of work.' She arranged her lipsticked mouth into a wide smile and tilted her head slightly to one side.

'Margaret, stop it,' I said. 'He's a friend of mine.'

'Sorry,' she said. 'No, really, I am interested. What are you working on at the moment?'

JJ looked a little confused, glancing at me for help.

I said, 'Go on, I'd like to know what's happening, then we can stop talking about work and get on to, I don't know, football or sex or something.'

'It's a bit sensitive, actually,' he began. 'Promise you're not a reporter and I might just talk.'

Margaret drew herself upright in her chair. 'I'm a poet,' she announced.

News to me, I thought. Is she trying to impress him?

'OK then – we've got a bit of a weird case just started,' JJ began, 'and for some reason we've been given practically no manpower and the amount of information coming in is non-existent. I've never seen an investigation take off so slowly. And it's a policeman who's been killed. I just don't understand it. It's as if there's some sort of cover-up going on or something. I don't know, either they think they know who it was or they don't really want to know.'

I was all ears, feeling almost unbearably tense, and it was fortunate that I'd told Margaret I was interested in the case because I found I couldn't speak to JJ about it. Not just yet. Margaret obligingly asked a few more questions. JJ tried to keep the conversation fairly general but I could see that he was interested in Margaret and she wasn't giving much away. A couple of drinks later, I knew almost everything there was to know about the progress of the investigation. To be fair, JJ hadn't been too indiscreet – there really wasn't much to tell.

Basically they had determined that the cause of death was repeated blows to the head, probably with a heavy cylindrical object. The time of death was estimated at between 6 p.m. and 10 p.m., and it was believed that some attempt had been made to conceal the body under rubbish bags. All personal belongings had been removed from the body, and there were puncture wounds to the torso, probably caused by broken glass, probably at the time of death or shortly after. Some house-to-house enquiries had been made with the owners of premises backing on to the alleyway but no one was surprised to learn that nobody had seen or heard anything unusual at any time during the evening. There had been several possible sightings of DCI

MacDonald, one as late as 9 p.m., and the team were now looking at questioning the prostitutes working in the area. The DCI's wife claimed he couldn't possibly have any enemies, except perhaps his girlfriend, whose name and phone number she'd supplied, and the girlfriend had said he probably had hundreds but she wasn't one of them, which rang true, since he was probably worth more to her and the kids alive than dead. She hadn't seen him after Tuesday afternoon and laughed bitterly at the idea he might have told her where he was going.

If what JJ said was true, there were fewer officers assigned to this case than to that of the burned woman found on the council estate. Which was very strange. JJ believed that there was something fishy going on, and that there was going to be some sort of cover-up. The area commander had been overheard speaking to the Assistant Chief Constable on the phone about it, and the overall impression was that there was some sort of unofficial investigation going on at an unusually high level. The opinion seemed to be that the less digging went on into the dead man's background and private life, the less eventual embarrassment would be caused to the force as a whole.

'So this is all unofficial and I'll deny telling you,' he warned, obviously remembering that Margaret wasn't even a police officer, 'and I'd rather you keep it to yourself.'

'Oh Margaret's the soul of discretion,' I reassured him. 'Sometimes people leave phone messages for me and she keeps them to herself for days.'

Margaret began to fidget, as well she might. A couple of months ago I'd been seeing the brother of a friend of mine, a lovely chap, it was all going really well until for no reason at all that I could see he stopped phoning, and I was thinking, what have I done wrong, did I call him the wrong name by mistake, have I shocked him with my strange habits or frightened him off somehow? Eventually I found out he'd rung three times and talked to Margaret, leaving messages twice and asking me to meet him once, all of which she'd forgotten to tell me until it was too late. So now his sister isn't so friendly either. Although I suppose if I'd been really keen on him, I might have rung him myself to find out what was going on.

It was getting towards closing time, the bar staff were bustling about, polishing glasses and empty-ing ashtrays and generally sending out subliminal sod-off-so-we-can-close-up messages and we began to think about going home.

To me JJ said, 'Are you going to the robbery squad do tomorrow night?' but I thought he was definitely interested in Margaret and really wanted to know if she would be there.

'We're thinking about it,' I said. 'Depends if I'm working on Saturday or not.'

'You should go if you can,' he told Margaret.

'They're always a laugh, the old rubbery squid nights out, and, you know, the more the merrier.'

He hurried off to get his train home. I've been to his house once, last year this was, for a barbecue. It was a very strange occasion, where I was the only person present who was not a policeman or a policeman's wife. Can't say I enjoyed it very much.

Very few of my colleagues live as centrally as I do – most of them like to get well away from the patch, out of London altogether, home to their wives and families in the country. For a few years. Then they start staying up in town more and more often. Policemen have a very high divorce rate. I'd never marry one, I know what they're like. Though I suppose I'd be as bad. To be fair, all police officers have a high divorce rate, not just the men. I've met quite a few colleagues' wives and it's always the same, they usually suspect me of having affairs with their husbands and you just can't say to these people – look, dearie, your 45-year-old husband is an overweight balding man who smokes Regal and eats pasties every day of his life; if he was the last man on earth, I'd be building a rocket; please ask yourself why a reasonably attractive woman like me would even consider a pig like your husband – because, believe me, I've tried, and they just take offence. Really, they do.

So Margaret and I finished our drinks and went home. Fed Cat, which deigned to lick the jelly off its catfood and left the rest as unfit for feline consumption. We painted our toenails, gold for me and blood red for Margaret. Ate ice cream picked up at the 7–11 on the way past, watched some telly, being deliberately girly.

'If I didn't know better,' said Margaret, 'I'd suspect you were maybe possibly, probably, almost definitely setting me up.'

'No way,' I answered. 'JJ's been a mate of mine for years, I wouldn't do that to him.'

'Ta very much.'

'Any time.'

So that was Thursday. Today. I'm all up to date now; here I am again at the computer on the dark wooden desk in my room, my custard-yellow bedroom at the top of the house. Across the road the last light has just gone out in the main bedroom of the house opposite. The chestnut tree outside my window blocks most of the noise from the street and the green and red curtains I made myself move slightly, although there's no discernible breeze. I can just hear Sinéad O'Connor wailing away in Margaret's sea-green room below, so I know she's still fretting over Jonathan.

No more energy to write today. I'm still not entirely sober and it's very late, but I think I'll have one last cold beer, and maybe, yes definitely, a hot bath.

It'll be easier in the morning.

Hothouse Flowers. Another of Margaret's favourites.

Wonder if JJ really told us everything. Wonder if he even knows everything. He isn't usually that talkative, he's more of your quiet, reserved, listen-a-lot chaps.

Phone rings at 0355 hrs. Nothing is said but I know it is Keith, having one of his bad days and wanting to share it. Margaret wanted us to get a new phone number but I wouldn't agree, so we compromise: she unplugs her phone when she goes to bed and I answer the out-of-hours calls. Which are all from Keith. He rings every couple of weeks in winter; less often in the summer. It has something to do with sunlight, I think, and as he's always been one to stay up all night, he gets deprived of natural light in the winter, whereas in summer he's less depressed. But as he hadn't been in touch for a while, I wasn't surprised to hear from him. Most people get a call in the middle of the night and automatically think the worst, fearing that someone has died or there's been an accident. I think, Oh, so Keith is still alive then. This time I can hear traffic in the background, so I guess he's in a phone box in central London somewhere. I can't hear him breathing. I say hello once and then wait. Eventually the phone is put down gently. I dial 1471. Yes, it's a payphone with an 0171 number. I ring it back in case he wants to talk but there is no answer, and although it takes me an hour to get back to sleep, it doesn't ring again.

I won't change the number because I feel guilty about breaking up with him. I know I'm not responsible for him but I can't bear to think he might phone at one of his low points and find the number had been changed. He can't really communicate when he's in one of those states but at least he can get in touch, have some sort of contact ...

Liaise with colleagues

NB: CRIMINAL LAW ACT 1977 S.4
You don't just have a social duty not to help criminals get away with it, you have a legal one too.

Friday morning not good. Not good at all. Very tired and slightly hungover. No dreams though; brain was clearly deadened by excess alcohol. What a good plan, I may try that again. Cat wanted out at 0527 hrs, then yowled outside to be let back in until

0715 hrs, when I got up. Relieved that there wasn't a hand-delivered note from Keith on the front mat – that's his other mode of communication and it upsets me and Margaret, the thought that he's been wandering round our house at night, putting notes through the letterbox, maybe sitting on the wall at the front talking to Cat, or in the back yard, maybe playing with matches ...

Dressed in only available clean clothes, heaped a pile of dirty ones in front of the washing machine in the hope that, as she works from home, Margaret might find time to bung them through for me, made mental note to buy tights at the 7–11, stole a peach and pineapple yogurt from Margaret, replaced empty carton at the back of the fridge, sneaked out of back door to avoid doubtless hungry cat, went to work. Forgot to buy tights, so had to keep on wearing emergency pair of thick brown runproofs kindly sent by mother last Christmas. Bloody things are indestructible.

Amazed to see Steady already in the office. He appeared to be going through the papers in my desk drawer, but claimed to have been looking for his A–Z. It turned out that he'd been kicked out by his girlfriend for some misdemeanour the night before – telling her he quite fancied her sister; I could have told him that's never a clever move, why are men so thick? – but had already told his wife he was staying in town, so he'd been kipping in the office and had just got up. He had a statement arranged for the afternoon and needed to check an address. I showed him his A–Z in its usual place on Julie's shelf beside the phone books. He looked a little sheepish and changed the subject, launching into the latest instalment of the life and times of a love-cheat detective.

According to Steady, his wife got used to him staying in town when he was on the headquarters surveillance team five years ago, and still thinks he works very late a couple of times a week. Personally I think she knows he's got a girlfriend and is secretly relieved not to have to see him every day. (I know I'd feel that way, but then I'd never have made the elementary error of having anything to do with him in the first place.) I have told him this theory a number of times but he doesn't agree.

Apart from getting a kick out of being unfaithful and getting away with it, he actually does think that he's completely irresistible to women. As a woman, I can state quite clearly that I find him completely unattractive. However, I've never had to check how resistible he might be, as he's obviously not interested in me, either. Last time someone from work asked me out for a drink – meaning, d'you want a shag? – was back when I was a uniformed PC and this bloke was my sergeant, a really slimy bloke with a silly bouffant hairstyle and shiny shoes. I waited until he'd asked me four times and rung me at home once and been told no way each time, and then told everyone I knew that I was being harassed by this married man and was considering ringing his wife to let her know. Didn't make an official complaint. Didn't have to. He never spoke to me again after that. Problem solved. As an added bonus, nobody at work has asked me out since. Strange, huh?

Steady says he's seen lampposts with better figures than me. I think he's intimidated by me because I've got a degree.

He produced a clean shirt from his voluminous sports bag and went off to shave.

Steady and I get on quite well now, although we didn't get off to a very good start when I joined the unit last year. I'm always a bit suspicious of people I don't know, and Steady's obnoxious to strangers and friends alike. After two days of relentless sexist jokes, all of which I ignored, he said to me, 'Don't you ever laugh or don't you think my jokes are funny?' To which I replied, 'Steadman, I find your jokes so funny I'm writing them all down.' So he walked in fear and dread of a grievance going in and Complaints and Discipline getting involved. Eventually I told him he was safe. We had an uneasy truce for a while, and although he still reminds me to go home at three o'clock to collect the kids from school, and expresses amazement whenever I manage to drive or park or put petrol into a car without crashing or crying, and always reminds me of the mirror-lipstick-manoeuvre rule when I set off anywhere by car, either I've mellowed over the past few months or he's not as bad as he used to be. He's clearly told his mates that I'm a lunatic feminist, though, as they're all extremely careful when I'm around, which I suspect amuses us both equally. His face lights up when anyone says anything particularly outrageous and he turns to me, waiting for the blistering reply. Half the time I can only be bothered because he so obviously expects it from me.

I had a quick look at the new general orders on my computer, to see who'd been posted where and which courses were coming up. Nothing of note – but I had messages, which I called up and read.

One was from Nina: 'Please contact custody asap ref. juvenile arrest', and was timed at 0635 hrs. The other was from DS Andrews, my old boss on the robbery squad, and read: 'Your presence required at Paddy's this evening due to expected consumption of lottery-funded beverages. Be there or we'll come round your house.' This was more than an idle threat. A few months ago they'd all turned up at my house, falling-down drunk and giggling at half past midnight, to see why I'd missed another of their drinks. Margaret was the only one at home, and being a hospitable soul, she'd let them in. I got in at one o'clock, having been at work for fifteen hours, to find my old boss and three colleagues slumped in the living room, looking at the photographs of me as a baby that Margaret had seen fit to produce by way of entertainment. As I said at the time, with friends like that, who needs friends? She said later by way of an excuse that the DS reminded her of a lecturer she'd gone out with in her first year at college. Not much of an excuse, but it was a bit of gossip she'd kept quiet at the time, so I had to forgive her.

Well, I had been planning to go to the do, anyway.

I rang Nina. She's the sergeant and had just started at 0600 hrs when one of the night-turn chaps, looking for a couple of hours' overtime, had brought in a twelve-year-old boy, arrested for being on enclosed premises. He'd broken into a restaurant and was found inside the walk-in fridge, stuffing his face as if he hadn't eaten for days. Turned out he hadn't – he was a runaway and he had refused all details at first. Nina'd left me the message in case he was 'one of ours', but in the meantime he'd given his name, a police-national-computer check had revealed him to be missing from a children's home in Dorset, and a pair of social workers were on their way to pick him up. I decided to pop down and talk to him, anyway; see how he'd managed to survive the big bad city by himself for the past few days.

I buzzed at the back door.

'Custody suite,' said Nina's voice.

'Chocolate pudding,' I replied.

'Enter, friend!'

Custody was quiet – there were a couple of wanted-on-warrants waiting to be collected for court, a suspected illegal immigrant waiting hopelessly for immigration officers, and the twelve-year-old, who was sitting across the desk from Nina eating a microwaved curry.

She said, 'Oh don't worry, Louisa, I've told the council and the inspector that we've got him. He's not going to come to any harm. I know he shouldn't be in here but they're cleaning out the juvenile detention room and you're quite happy, aren't you, Martin?'

The boy nodded but didn't reply, eyes down, busily tucking into the unappealing meal in front of him. He seemed to be enjoying it. Children are strange.

I decided to leave him to it for the moment. 'Martin, I'm from the Child Protection Unit, my name's Louisa and I'd like to talk to you in a minute,' I said to him, 'once you've finished breakfast, OK?'

He nodded his grubby head, looked up and caught my eye, nearly smiled.

Nina called her gaoler through and asked him to put the kettle on.

'What's the news then?' she asked. 'Have they narrowed the field of suspects for the DCI's murder, or is it still the husband of any woman who's ever worked with him?'

'Don't be so unimaginative,' I said. 'Could be a woman that did it. Or a child, a team of acrobats, a specially trained monkey. Actually, I don't think they're putting too much effort into this one – I wouldn't be too surprised if the final verdict isn't suicide.'

'Yeah right,' she said, unimpressed. 'Like he suddenly felt guilty for his past years of bad behaviour, dragged himself up an alley round the back of King's Cross and smacked himself over the head with a bloody great cosh. And you call yourself a detective . . .'

'Well, whatever, I was talking to someone on the team, and –'

'Wonder who that was?' interrupted Nina. 'Could my source be correct in reporting that you were having a cosy little tête-à-tête in the Stag last night with a certain tall, well-dressed, ginger-headed detective?'

'As I was saying, I was talking to someone on the team and they're really struggling,' I said, 'and no, it wasn't a cosy little anything. I think he fancies my housemate, if you must know.'

'Shame,' said Nina, raising one eyebrow comically, 'you'd make such a funny couple.'

I resisted the temptation to demand an explanation for this remark, maintaining a dignified silence. Couldn't think who could have seen us, either, it is not a popular pub with most of the ones from work – not enough young women in there on the average night – but I knew if I asked Nina, she'd think I was showing signs of being defensive. A schoolgirl error. No way.

The gaoler returned with a couple of styrofoam cups of coffee.

The runaway Martin scraped the last grain of rice from the corner of his dish and then told me that he'd been looked after by a couple of older girls, in their late teens he thought, who were living under Waterloo Bridge and had adopted him on his first evening in London. They'd fed him, showed him how to beg and keep an eye out for the Old Bill at the same time, taken him round central London, pierced his ear for him and lent him a sleeping bag. He'd managed to get himself lost the night before, after they'd all gone into Soho to beg off the tourists, and couldn't find his way back to them. Not wanting to ask anyone for directions for fear of showing himself to be a stranger, he'd simply climbed in through the first forceable window he'd found. He'd run away from the home after an argument with a member of staff, but was quite happy to go back. Four days away in London would make him a hero with his other inmates and he was looking forward to telling them a few tall stories.

Nina got the gaoler to treat his pierced, and by now, swollen ear with an antiseptic wipe, gave him a lecture on the dangers of roaming round London at his age and told him to wash his face and hands. He did as he was told, and was rewarded with a brief hug before she sent him off to the detention room to sleep until his social workers turned up.

'Bloody kids,' she said. 'I love them but I couldn't eat a whole one.'

I flicked through the last few custody records, and quickly spotted a couple of familiar names.

'I see that Alison's still getting arrested with startling frequency,' I remarked casually, 'but I'm surprised she's been done for affray – she's usually pretty quiet.'

'Yes, I saw that – she was kicked out before I came on duty,' replied Nina, 'but I think it was over a fight with some other tom. We've been told to ask all the local prostitutes about the other night. You know – where were you on the night of Tuesday to Wednesday, who were you with, what did you see? and so on. I dread to think what some of the answers will be. Can you imagine if they take that literally – can't see how a blow-by-blow, oops, sorry, detailed account of the local prostitutes' movements will help the investigation. Anyway, they've given us the incident room number in case anyone has anything useful to say. No doubt the chaps will be eagerly awaiting our calls. Hope they're only submitting relevant statements, otherwise some bastard on the murder squad will be getting off on all this.'

I didn't want to show my unease – Nina's very sharp – but I managed a cynical laugh and was relieved when we got off the subject.

She told me in great detail and with obvious enjoyment a story I'd heard before as a rumour but had never had confirmed about one of the other Custody sergeants, a bully of a bloke who thought women couldn't do the job properly. One night a few months earlier he'd given the cell keys to a drunk-in-a-public-place he was kicking out at three in the morning. The still-not-entirely-sober old gent staggered off up the road and the potentially disastrous error was only discovered twenty minutes later when he'd returned to bang his fists persistently on the steel outer door. The gaoler had gone out to tell him to shut the fuck up or go back in the cell, at which point he'd protested, 'But I've only come to give you these back, they were in my property bag but they're not mine.'

The rumble of a diesel van engine, followed by a sudden burst of noise outside the back door, signalled the arrival of a pair of rumpled and harassed-looking uniformed officers dragging a fighting drunk into the Custody area.

Nina sighed. 'So much for my quiet morning,' she said, reaching behind her for a fresh custody sheet. 'Beats me how these people manage to get drunk before breakfast. Do they start early or carry on late?'

I waved a cheery goodbye as the drunk was slung, still shouting obscenities, into the nearest cell and Nina started to list his property.

Items retained by police: one bic lighter, one penknife, one belt, one metal fork, one length of wire, one empty whiskey bottle, one box safety matches.

Items retained by prisoner: 10 Bensons, £0.33, one illustrated Bible.

Instead of returning to my office, I sat in the canteen for a while, trying to think what Maria and Alison were likely to say when questioned. I'd tried to get information out of women like them before, often without much success. It would not be in their interests to get involved, unless they thought they were suspects themselves. They certainly wouldn't want to make formal statements, as they'd be extremely unwilling to have to go to court as witnesses. I hoped that whoever was asking the questions managed to miss the point somehow. Or else got their backs up so that they would be uncooperative. Might as well face it. I had no idea what they would say. Most likely they'd simply say they couldn't remember anything unusual about the evening (which was probably the case, why would they?) and leave it at that.

Back in the office Julie and Steady were both engrossed in paperwork.

Steady was preparing his fantasy football team for the coming season, covering sheets of paper with imaginary teams. I noticed that despite professing to follow Millwall, he hadn't chosen any of their players. Apparently this just showed how little I understood about football, being a girl, something to do with leagues or divisions being beyond my limited powers of comprehension. I left him alone.

Julie was writing out a report requesting additional manpower and vehicles for an operation she planned to run in September, once the autumn school term had started.

Both acknowledged my return, Julie with a wave of her Biro, Steady by holding out a torn-off piece of paper. It was a message from the DI in charge of Candy's case, asking me to page her when convenient. Couldn't be anything too urgent, then. DIs usually want paging asap. I have had very little input on the investigative side of this case – I can't get involved, my role is to look after the victim and get her through the court case to a point where she can eventually get some counselling. This can't begin until after the verdict.

There are new rules and regulations and guidelines coming in to change the system, but it all takes time and nobody really knows how to interpret the new ideas, so everyone's too scared of getting it wrong to change from the accepted practices. Really, the child victim of an attack like this one should make a statement on video, with a trained police officer and a trained social worker present, in which every detail is covered and all the relevant questions are asked. Then the child should be able to receive counselling and hopefully work towards resuming a normal life. The video would then be played in court and the child would not be required to give evidence, whether by video link or in person, at all.

But what about the accused's rights; what about the cross-examination every defence barrister relies upon? Obviously, at the outset of the investigation I couldn't even associate with the investigative team. Until the video statement was made with the description of the man involved, and so on, I would be accused by any eventual defence of planting ideas in Candy's head, giving her a description to fit a suspect we already had. They made up an E-fit picture based on descriptions given by the children who had been with Candy when the man approached her, which again I couldn't see in case of evidence contamination. The problem being, that the great British public are only too willing to believe that all coppers are bent and will do anything to ensure a conviction. So in the days after the attack and before the arrest, I had no idea how the enquiry was progressing. In actual fact the man was arrested within the week, his girlfriend agreed to stand as witness against him and everything should have been done and dusted months ago. Except the man knows how to manipulate the system, and he's been given every opportunity to do so, to prevent him having possible grounds for an appeal later.

So anyway, I phoned DI Williams, who turned out to be making a welfare check, expecting the trial to progress on Monday as scheduled. Apparently the pre-trial arguments had ended the previous evening, with some evidence being excluded due to procedural errors. Fortunately much of the excluded material was circumstantial and not really central to the prosecution case. There remained a huge amount of evidence against the man, from the identification parades, the house searches, the testimony of his former girlfriend. On some days I couldn't see why he had to have a trial at all, being quite so clearly guilty.

I'd arranged to take Candy to the court buildings that afternoon, to show her round and get her used to the atmosphere, take her to the special room where we would spend most of the next week. Of course, she's getting to be an old hand at all this, having had the same tour of another crown court building last time round. Still, it was worth doing again. If only to get me out of the office, and out of the building. Funny that I've never thought before how weird it is, working in a building full of people busy finding things out. Oh, not in a logical, sensible well-organised, efficient way, but still, so many people working away must get results from time to time ... and now the thought makes me feel almost ill.

Before meeting Candy, I had to deal with my other message – a note on my desk asking me to contact the incident room re. the MacDonald murder. Not a phone call I fancied making. Maybe they thought I could be of some assistance. Eventually I picked up the phone and dialled the internal number. Apparently his wife had initially refused to talk to anyone on the investigating team, had then mentioned various strange goings-on in the past few months, and finally agreed to meet the DS with her solicitor present. I was asked to speak to the MacDonalds' two daughters to see if they could shed any light on what had been happening.

I made tentative arrangements to see them at their home one evening early in the next week.

Effective communication

NB: SEXUAL OFFENCES ACT 1956, SECTION 4 (1)
It is indeed a wicked and evil thing to do, to administer alcohol or drugs to a woman in order for someone to have intercourse with her. It is, however, OK in law to do this to a man, but for best results you do have to judge the quantities you administer rather finely. Or so I'm told.

I collected Candy from school and drove her straight to the court. She's always disappointed that

I drive an unmarked car – she'd rather travel with lights and sirens on, speeding through the traffic instead of crawling along as we did. At least the car I'd been given – heavy old Rover, though it was – had a police radio installed, so we drove along listening to the busy airwaves. There were stop checks being done, information was being passed about break-ins and domestics, shoplifters were detained and disturbances caused and then calmed. Candy wanted to have a go on the radio herself but agreed to wait until another day. I rarely use the radio, even though you are supposed to book on and off whenever you drive anywhere – my theory is, if they know where you are, they won't leave you alone. Safer to maintain radio silence. Candy saw the logic of that.

She turned up her nose at the poky children's room, with its shabby collection of cuddly toys and bright posters on the walls, drank a large coke in the canteen, complained about the scratchy toilet paper in the ladies', held my hand in the corridors and on the wide staircase and eventually decided that she wasn't scared of the court buildings.

I dropped her off at home and returned the car to the yard by 1800 hrs. Filled in the log book, which was a couple of hundred miles out as usual. Work over. Playtime.

I decided not to bother going home to change – there's nobody at work I want to impress and I feel as if I'm in drag on the rare occasions when I do make an effort to dress up.

The robbery squad were having their social gathering in a noisy Irish bar called Paddy McGill's, a slightly seedy place which happens to stay open late several nights a week in the name of entertainment, providing a range of deedly-deedly-dee type bands which are usually (thankfully) inaudible beneath the din of beer-fuelled conversation. When there isn't a band on, the juke box is excellent, with a range of Irish, country and western, and odd tunes rarely found together. The tables and stools are low and made of dark wood, with grubby red velvet settees along the walls and a fine selection of tattooed students and long-haired labourers scattered around them. Makes me feel old sometimes – when I was a student, it was the labourers who had tattoos and the students had long hair. I told this to Steady once, and he went off into the usual spiel about me being over thirty, starting to sag and therefore being desperate to get a man and have some kids. I said having kids was all very well, but illegal if they were under sixteen.

Paddy's is rumoured to be a bit of a drugs pub, but we've been promised by the drug squad that we'll get twenty minutes' warning if they want to raid it while we're in there. I have to admit that I have noticed that the studenty types do tend to disappear into huddles near the toilet entrances from time to time and often seem out of their heads after very small quantities of beer, but hey, that's not my area of knowledge, and until such time as I get sent on a drugs buyer's course, I'm not going to get involved off duty.

Tonight's do was in honour of a prolific if inept robber from Nunhead called Vincent Allan Ross, a 26-year-old, unemployed, unskilled, illiterate chap with a bad stutter who admitted five knife-point robberies, two thefts and an attempt at Inner London Crown Court earlier in the week. In interview his reply to the allegations put to him was 'Oh come on, are you having a l-l-laugh? You know me, I'm a b-b-b-burglar not a r-r-robber, just l-l-look at my form, it weren't me. Now can I go, please. I have to c-c-cash my giro before the p-p-post office shuts, I owe m-my m-m-mum the money and she'll k-k-kill me if I don't get her it tod-d-day.' His change of plea from not guilty to a full and open confession part way through his trial was rewarded with the reduced sentence of five years' imprisonment.

Beers all round for a job well done. Although, if you ask me, every time you put away a robber you create a job opportunity.

The robbery squad don't like to hide their lights under bushels, and tend to circulate news of their successful cases via invitations to their celebratory drinks. By the time I got to the pub just after seven there was a crowd there already, some of them obviously having popped in at lunch time and not made it back to work. Well, it's too risky to go back to work these days if you have accidentally had three or four too many. Much better to ring in and say you're out taking statements – a handy phrase, easily condensed to OTS, although this can also be interpreted as 'over the side'. Indeed, many people make the most of the ambiguity of it all.

The main group was congregated towards the front of the pub, backs to the wall with a view of the door, in the almost regulation garb of jeans, designer T-shirt and fleece jacket, so much in favour in plain clothes circles, or the more traditional, old-fashioned dark suits, white shirts and flashy ties still worn by headquarters, officebound types. The robbery squad do sometimes dress up like the robbers they deal with, mainly to annoy them, I believe, in Moschino or Versace jeans and brightly coloured YSL shirts, but not on this occasion.

I contributed my tenner to the beer glass stuffed with notes on the table, selected a couple of notes and struggled to the bar to order the next round, doing my usual impressive trick of remembering what everyone drinks. All these years on and I can still do the waitress thing – I never forget who takes milk and sugar in what, or who drinks Guinness or bottled lager instead of the more usual pint-of-best.

Apart from Steady, who was probably only killing time until his current girlfriend finished work at the trendy café in Covent Garden which she runs, most of them would still be there drinking at last orders. And he'd still be there if she hadn't forgiven him yet. I promised myself I would make an effort to stay relatively sober and go home reasonably early.

DC Bell was recounting his afternoon's work in the witness box prior to the guilty plea, during which the defence tried to get him to admit that he knew the accused was elsewhere on the occasion of at least one of the robberies. Apparently at the time of one of Ross's robberies there was a report of an attempted robbery at a shopping centre in south-east London, for which the victim had eventually withdrawn his statement, and they were trying to use this as an alibi – an original if flawed strategy.

DC Hadley chipped in with a story about the inspector running one of the ID parades coming to blows with a solicitor in the corridor, and the rest of the robbery squad were also talking job.

DS Andrews asked me to tell the one about when I was being questioned by a clever-clever defence barrister about how I knew that his client had committed a particular robbery from the description given.

I'd said, 'From what the lady told me and the description she gave, I just knew it was him.'

He said, 'What do you mean, you just knew?'

I said, 'Will you accept the definition of knowledge as justified true belief with no false lemmas?'

He decided he had no further questions at that time.

It is not often you get the chance to do that.

Someone continued the theme with the story

about the PC giving evidence in a speeding case, where the defendant had been seen by two constables driving his Mercedes in excess of fifty miles an hour in a thirty-mile-an-hour zone. The defence brief threw a fountain pen across the court and asked the PC to estimate its speed of travel if he was so good at it, to which he replied, 'Well, obviously, I've never driven one of those, but' – at which point general laughter ensued until the judge restored order and asked the barrister to refrain from such pointless theatricals in his court in future.

There was some discussion of who was likely to get the open DCI job now that DCI MacDonald wasn't in a position to do it. Someone had heard a rumour that the job would be going to one of the two female chief inspectors currently looking to move into CID, with popular opinion favouring Judy Carr, who had recently come out as a lesbian and was known to be living with one of the female trainers from the force training school. It was generally believed that she had come out in a cynical attempt to force a promotion on the assumption that the job would be too scared of an allegation of discrimination on grounds of sexual orientation to do anything other than promote her at the first available opportunity. And there were a couple of lighthearted suggestions that the unfortunate demise of DCI MacDonald could turn out to be the first in a series of many to come, paving the way for a whole range of new promotion opportunities. I was quite attracted to the notion of a crack team of women secretly assassinating the more overtly sexist policemen of rank, and agreed that if such a movement existed, I'd put my name down right away. We do talk some nonsense in the pub.

However, just then I wanted a change of subject. Fortunately Margaret showed up, all smiles and dangly earrings, wearing a stretchy pink dress over paisley-patterned leggings, her hair piled on top of her head and decorated with a sunflower. She poured a fistful of pound coins into the kitty, explaining that instead of going to the cashpoint, she'd emptied out all her handbags and coat pockets and found twenty-six pounds in change.

'How long have you been here?' she asked.

'About two pints,' I said.

'Oh good, so I'm not late then.'

I did a few brief introductions. She'd met some of the robbery squad the year before, when I was working with them, and had let some of the others into the house late that night. I'm not sure, but I think I may have introduced her once as 'the woman I live with' and this may explain the various winks, nods and half-smily glances that greeted her arrival. Could just have been her clothes, though. I have become a more conventional dresser, recently, mainly to reassure the families of the children I work with, but Margaret still wears the clothes we used to buy in the market when we were students. She thinks that her favourite bits of clothing are bound to look good together because she likes them all separately.

DS Andrews gave her a hug, which surprised her, but not the rest of us. He's got divorced lately and obviously feels short on physical contact these days. Margaret freed herself and we made a quick trip across the crowded pub to the jukebox for some old favourites. 'Stand by Your Man', 'Jolene', 'The Irish Rover', considered the Commitments but decided in favour of the Undertones, slapped on a bit of Van Morrison for good measure and sat back down.

There was some rearrangement of tables and seats and I found myself between Nina and Steady, who were happily exchanging insults. Nina's new man wasn't coming this evening, seemed that he hadn't got on with her colleagues last week and wouldn't be persuaded to try again, so she was telling Steady in minute detail how much better this new man was in bed than Steady had been the one time they'd ended up together after a previous robbery squad drink. This was all news to me, but explained their half-joking, half-antagonistic re-lationship. Steady was protesting that he'd had to get so drunk to face sleeping with her that his performance had been impaired, and she was dropping peanuts into his beer, and there wasn't much I could contribute to the conversation. Look-ing round, I saw that JJ was at the bar and I waved him over, moving up along the wooden bench so he could slide in next to me.

'I see that Margaret made it,' he said.

'Listen,' I said, 'the robbery squad think I live with her.'

'Yeah well, you do.'

'Yeah, but not like that. You know, they think we're together ...'

'Excellent!' he said. 'Can I come home with the pair of you and really start a rumour?'

Margaret swapped seats with Nina and joined in. 'Please don't spoil it,' she said. 'I've told Steady the only reason I won't shag him is because he's not a woman.'

We all laughed at the idea of Steady as a woman. Ugh. Although, to be honest, he is one of those blokes who need a bra more than I do.

More beer arrived. Familiar faces came and went. I listened to conversations about work, drinking exploits, drinking exploits at work, scandalous and mostly untrue gossip and rumour, and the odd mention of our dead colleague. Mainly, I kept my mouth shut. Fortunately I often do. I'm known as a good listener.

I remember the whole table singing along to 'Mustang Sally' and 'Sometimes It's Hard to Be a Woman'; I may even have joined in, but I think the general noise would have covered my dreadful singing voice. A band came on towards eleven o'clock and belted out a noisy and enthusiastic set, finishing with the Buzzcocks' 'Ever Fallen in Love', which got everyone singing again, before retiring to the bar and demanding many pints of Guinness.

At some stage I remembered the first part of my promise to myself. I knew there were two things I meant to do, but I just couldn't remember the second. Couldn't find Margaret. Couldn't remember if I'd told her what I was trying to remember. There didn't seem to be much point in keeping only one promise out of two. Wondered if she'd disappeared with the DS. Well, at least he was technically single these days. I remember moving to a quieter area at the back of the pub for privacy during a long and hilarious conversation with Nina, in which we were trying to put all the men we'd ever had any sort of relationship with into order of merit based on a complicated points system. Not an easy process at the soberest of times, even when you narrow it down to your top ten, all time favourites. Then Nina disappeared to the loo and never came back. I drank some more beer, switched to whiskey when I was too bloated to swallow any more gassy pints, and finally staggered out of the pub as it was closing. Realised I was drunk, which for some reason came as something of a surprise. Still couldn't find Margaret. Got a taxi home, concentrating hard on staying awake. Well, you never know with these taxi drivers.

Lights were on in the living room, television flickering light and floor lamp. I did the usual 'Oh shit, hope Keith hasn't let himself in while I'm out' panic-and-freeze thing, but calmed down when I realised there was no tobacco smell in the air. And anyway, he would have probably sat there in the dark rather than have advertised his presence. Wished I'd managed to get his keys off him when he left, but it seemed more important to get rid of him without a fight at the time. No, there was definitely no rollie smoke in the hall, why am I so paranoid? Margaret must be home. Wondered when she sloped off and why she didn't tell me she was leaving. Couldn't be bothered to speak to her – needed to get to bed. How did that quotation go – 'when the singing was sung and the dancing was done they began to think kindly of their beds . . .'? I couldn't quite recall how it went so resolved to look it up tomorrow. Thought kindly of my bed, always there when I need it, never lets me down. Chucked a handful of dried cat food out of the back door in case Margaret didn't get round to letting Cat in. Up the wooden hill to Bedfordshire.

Dreamed I was in a cavernous building, like a sort of Hollywood medieval castle, all echoing corridors and huge empty rooms opening off on either side. There were winding staircases and it was cool and draughty; I heard footsteps and voices far off but never met anyone. I was trying to get somewhere in the building, completely lost but felt quite safe, walking along by myself through deep shadows and ill-lit passageways. There were lights on here and there, some in character, torches stuck into brass holders high on the walls, some unexpected, a streetlight found in a corner, orange neon bulb flickering. Finally I saw a desk at the end of a long open room, with a figure bent over papers and heavy leather bound ledgers, and as I got closer it became Steady. I recognised the way his hair flops over his forehead and he looked up and saw me and nodded as if he had been expecting me, and maybe he had. He said, 'Take the third exit and just keep going until you get there, it's not that much further on.' Then he bent over his work again, and suddenly I was happy, no longer anxious, because I knew that although there was still a long way to go, I'd get there eventually. I didn't mind how long it took – it wasn't as if I was in a hurry.

Relationships with others

NB: CONSPIRACY TO PERVERT THE COURSE OF
JUSTICE
*Lots of policemen wind up in court facing this sort
of charge, generally when they are thought to have
lied about something important.*

Saturday, usually a rest day. I was not officially at
work but I was supposed to be taking Candy out for
the afternoon. Woke up late; wondered if I'd make
it. Wasted half an hour wondering. Couldn't decide

137

what to wear. Stumbled out of bed in a rush, reluctant to leave the warmth of my duvet. Grabbed comforting fluffy dressing gown, clutched it to my chest and staggered down the top flight of stairs, clinging to the rickety banisters for support, pushed open bathroom door, rubbing puffy eyes and started to head through Radox-scented steam towards basin. Surprised to see that the body in the bath wasn't familiar blond Margaret but large pale male. Large pale freckly ginger male. More surprised to find that I wasn't happy with this. Temporarily abandoned any plans I might have had to transform myself into a recognisable human being, mumbled unfriendly greeting, 'Morning' , stumbled back to bedroom, collapsed on bed. Curled up round pillow. Head hurt. Eyes hurt. Hair felt sticky, skin felt too thin. Teeth felt soft. Bones were far too heavy, was that a recognised disease? No, that is brittle bone disease, stupid ... Eventually, bathwater gurgling sounds and heavy foot noises signalled a free bathroom. At least he has been properly brought up, he'd cleaned the bath out. (I checked, no curly ginger hairs anywhere.) Splashed face, combed hair, brushed teeth.

Inspecting the bath reminded me of a man I came across once, a six-foot-four ginger flasher – easy enough to find him as it happened, he was well known to several collators and still lived at a previous address – but, anyway, he decided to dye his hair so as to be less immediately recognisable by the police. Trouble was, every time he dropped his pants he gave himself away.

Teapot-lid banging and cutlery-on-plate noises in the kitchen, so I decided against breakfast. Risky, anyway, in my state. Even half a glass of water felt decidedly brave, but it stayed down. That must have been a good sign. Found bag, keys, money, warrant card, travel pass. Called out 'Bye' as I slammed the front door; stamped towards tube station.

Cheered up enough on tube to hum 'Happy Loving Couples' to myself. Realised I was annoying the couple in the seats opposite. Cheered up even more.

Arrived early at Candy's mother's house. The baby was crying, the eldest daughter hadn't got home from a rave the night before, one of the boy's friends had been staying overnight and had wet the bed, as had Candy. She always does. There was nothing for lunch and everyone was annoyed with everyone else. Mother's boyfriend was slightly pissed, arguing loudly with anyone who would answer him through the open door while drinking cider from a two-litre plastic bottle on the front step as I arrived. Everything in the garden was dead or dying, even the shabby privet hedge had given up, the path was cracking up and the steps were crumbling. Ants rushed about. A large black and brown slobbery dog was drinking water from a mug without a handle. Situation normal.

Reminded me of a house I went into once with a social worker. She'd contacted me because there were children at risk and on her last visit she'd told the parents they'd have to clean up or the kids would be taken away. When I went with her, the mother was on her knees in the bathroom scrubbing away at the filthy toilet bowl, which her husband had pulled away from the wall and put into the bath for her to wash.

Collected Candy and left the rest of them to it. You can't save them all.

She was starving, so we picked up a pizza and a couple of milkshakes and went to eat in the park. Sun not too hot, gentle breeze and I was starting to feel better. Saved our crusts to throw to the ducks and geese, had an ice cream. Some days I can almost imagine having kids myself, maybe a small dark-eyed girl, a real tomboy, racing round on skates or wobbling down the road on a bike with stabilisers. Most days I admit that I don't really like them very much. Never picked up much of a maternal vibe when I was a child. A friend of mine at university did seven years of medicine before she admitted to herself and the world at large that she really hates sick people. She's a gardener now, works for the council.

Well, you don't have to like kids to try and get some of the people who hurt them locked up. Probably helps not to get too involved.

Candy wanted to go on the swings but doesn't

know the kids playing there, so she just watches instead, wistful but too shy to intrude. It occurred to me that I'm nearly as old as her mother. Scary thought.

Dropped her home, explained that I couldn't stop for a cuppa – which I'd have had to make for them, and there wouldn't have been any washing up liquid and the milk would have been off or absent and I'd have felt awkward but been unable to bring myself to drink out of the grimy cup. Took myself back home.

Empty house. Someone had tidied away the kitchen things into a tidy pile by the sink, all the downstairs curtains had been pulled back and the living room table had been wiped. Smart. There was a note on the kitchen worktop – I thought it was from Margaret but turned out to be from JJ. Realised he'd probably tidied up too. Hoped he didn't find anything too incriminating in the living room or anywhere else for that matter. 'LOUISA – RING ME THIS AFTERNOON, PLEASE. I NEED TO TALK TO YOU XXX JJ.'

Yeah great, I thought, where was he last night when I might have wanted to talk to him? But at a loose end, and wanting to find out what was going on with him and Margaret, knowing he'd tell me and she probably wouldn't, I phoned him.

'Hello?'

'Hi JJ, it's me, Louisa.'

'Ah, yeah, thanks for phoning, um, sorry about

this morning.'

'No, I'm sorry I walked in on you, it didn't occur to me to knock.'

Pause.

'So how are you today? Hungover?' he said.

'Not too bad now. I've been in the park, fed the ducks. I'm OK. You?'

'I've got a headache the size of Australia, and I can't look at the light, otherwise I'm fine.'

'So what do you want to talk about?'

'Oh, the note I left ... Well, it's kind of difficult really. Look, maybe this can wait. What are you working on on Monday?'

'Court all week.'

'Right. It's about work – I kept trying to talk to you at the do but you were flirting with people all night, then I thought you'd gone and Margaret said she hadn't seen you for ages, either, so I brought Margaret home. She wasn't feeling too well by this stage, and then when we got in there was no mineral water left but we found that bottle of lemon vodka in the freezer and it seemed like a good idea at the time ... She went on and on about some bloke called Jonathan, asked me loads of questions I couldn't answer about the robbery squad DS and then staggered off to bed. Then, well, it is all a blur for a while. I know I really tried to stay awake until you got in, but you know how it is. I think I must have passed out on the sofa. Anyway, I woke up feeling really rough and freezing cold at four in the morning and I could hardly breathe, itchy face and so on – the cat was lying on my chest and I think I must be allergic to it, so I put it out and grabbed a couple of coats off the back of the door and got back to sleep.'

Sounded plausible to me. Felt oddly light-hearted.

After a short pause JJ spoke again and there was a change in his voice. I have never heard him so hesitant. 'Shit, Lou, I don't know how to say this, but you know I'm collating and inputting on the MacDonald case?'

'Yes?'

'Do you remember talking to a prostitute called Alison on Tuesday?'

'Aren't you supposed to caution me first?' I couldn't believe I was joking about this.

'Look, she's given a statement mentioning you and a bloke who sounds like Fraser Mac, and I don't know whether I should tell you this but I was thinking about how strained you've been looking this week. Margaret reckons you've been acting weird at home as well. We've both been worried, so I don't know why I did this but I never listed it and I've gone and fed it to Sammy Shredder.'

'You've what?'

This was so unlikely, coming from JJ, the only person I know who never cheated on his fitness test in training school, who always had his pocket note-book up to date, who never ever did anything wrong.

'I've lost the statement. Nobody else will miss it. I mean, the girl's obviously lying but the last thing you need at a time like this is some arse trying to fit you up to get a clear-up.'

I tried to make sense of this. 'Whaddaya mean, at a time like this?' I asked suspiciously.

'Oh, sorry. Margaret told me a few things that maybe she shouldn't have. Sorry, Lou, I'll keep it to myself. I promise. But if you ever need to talk, you know my number.'

'Thanks, I'll bear it in mind ... I've got to go, JJ, things to sort out, you know ...'

'OK. Well, see you around ...'

'Bye ...'

Several things needed thinking about here.

1 What has Margaret told him?
2 Why has she told him whatever she's told him?
3 Why has he done this for me?
4 Why am I so pleased that he's done this for me?
5 What am I going to do now?
6 How can I cope with the week ahead?
7 What am I going to do about Candy?
8 How am I going to face the two MacDonald daughters?
9 How can I find out what is happening at work when I'm in court?
10 Why do all the above seem so trivial compared to the fact that JJ's put his job at risk for me?

Obviously the first thing to do was have a long talk with Margaret, see what she knew.

Saturday afternoon and I knew she was officially not speaking to Jonathan, although I suspected she'd probably told him she spent last night with another man in case he'd get jealous, so she would probably be out shopping. Hoped she was out food shopping, we were all out of treats and snacks.

As if by magic, I heard her key in the door and went to let her in. She was struggling with four plastic bags – she'd been to the supermarket, the offie and the market. God, I loved this woman.

Margaret arranged fruit in the bowl, complaining that she'd been palmed off with over-ripe, squashy bananas, and as for the rest of it, 'The oranges are tiny and I've never felt a mango so hard ...'

We collapsed with raucous laughter, recovered momentarily, caught each other's eye, collapsed again. This was why I didn't live by myself; apart from the rent, of course, it is the companionship that is so important.

We chucked tins into cupboards, I put the kettle on, Margaret ripped open a packet of chocolate Hobnobs and we slouched into the living room for a good long girlie chat. I poured out our tea – mine, very strong, with a drop of milk; Margaret, weak, without. We took a few biscuits and settled into the cushions. I put on an old Elvis Costello CD and the windows were open, letting a slight breeze wave the creamy curtains. Kids were playing an excitable game of cricket in the street; Cat was keeping an eye on them from the windowsill. Lazy afternoon.

Margaret leapt straight to the point. 'So what's going on with you and JJ?'

'I could ask you the same thing,' I replied.

'Look, he spent all night talking about you, stupid. So go on, tell me what's going on.'

'I wish I knew,' I said. 'He's been my friend for six years and suddenly I don't know how I feel about him ... but I want to see him all the time and when I see him I want to touch him all the time, and I don't dare say anything in case I've made it up all by myself and he's still just thinking of me as a friend. So what was he saying about me, how come he came home with you last night, what went on before I got home, where did he sleep, where did you sleep, what is happening, Margaret?'

Margaret sat up very straight-backed and crossed her legs in what looked like a yoga position. 'Like I said, we talked about you. The man's crazy about you, I think he has been for years. I mean, he didn't exactly say so, of course, but d'you remember telling him about when you were breaking up with Keith? When he was threatening to kill himself if you didn't love him any more, saying stuff about burning the house down and that sort of thing? Well, JJ was telling me how much he wanted to go round and beat him up for you, but thought you'd be cross with him if he did. Like, he wanted to look after you when you were so upset, but he thought

146

you'd tell him to fuck off if he offered.'

This was suddenly exactly what I'd been needing to hear, troubling and complicating though it was. I knew that this was another thing to worry about – I'd have to be even more careful. It's one thing trying to survive by yourself and another thing trying to make sure someone else survives with you. Should I tell him everything or anything, would he want to know, will he still want to know me if he does know. If I didn't tell him what would I tell him? But at the same time I was just sitting there with a big smile on my face, and Margaret was grinning back at me.

'I knew it,' she said. 'I knew it as soon as I saw your face when he turned up in the pub. You looked like yourself for the first time in days.'

And I remembered what JJ said on the phone. 'What did you tell him?' I asked, 'He was going on about the hard time I'm having, and I didn't know what was supposed to have happened.'

Margaret bit her fingernail, peeling silver varnish hanging off in a strip. 'Well, Lou, I can't remember all that much about last night, but I do know I thought I should tell him something. He'd noticed you were being a bit odd and was asking me when it started and what you'd been like at home, and I'm supposed to be your best friend, so what am I supposed to say, she hasn't told me, either? So I said you were really upset over the Candy thing, and worried about your new boss, and thinking of getting a new job, and generally stressed out, and that Keith's been ringing in the middle of the night threatening to kill himself ... You know, the usual stuff.'

I thought about this. Yes, it did sound like plenty of stress to be going on with, and I wondered why I hadn't cracked up weeks ago. Yet there I was, still struggling on despite the other, more pressing reason for my recent absentmindness and preoccupation. Could I just give up and walk away? Could I confess and plead temporary insanity due to stress coupled with self-defence and ... no, no, no, no, no. The problem with reasonable force is that it has to be reasonable, and if I can't remember, how can I find out?

None of this was helping any.

Nothing had really changed, except that JJ had risked his job to help me out because he loved me. Or maybe just fancied me. I didn't know ... But I did know that he will wish he hadn't – his conscience will trouble him. But, then again, he didn't know what I'd done.

Margaret was still waiting for a response.

'Sorry if I've been a bit distant, it has all been getting to me recently,' I said.

'Yeah, I know, but just look forward to the holiday.'

'Have you spoken to that Jonathan?' I asked, needing to change the subject and realising that I'm not the only one with problems.

'Not a peep out of him since he went away,' said Margaret. 'But I haven't really missed him, you know. I think he's a lot less interesting than he thinks he is and I wish I'd realised earlier. Although he did have the best lines – you know, he told me once he loved my body because of all the amazing shapes in it? Anyway, I'm considering my options. I had an interesting offer last night too.'

I thought privately that Margaret was probably the only woman I knew who would like that line. I raised a questioning eyebrow and waited to see if she would volunteer any more about the recent offer. She didn't.

We went through the holiday brochures again and decided that the easiest thing to do was to go to the same place we went to before – not very adventurous, but it was quite last-minute and we hadn't got time to do any research. Margaret asked if I wanted to invite JJ and I pointed out that we hadn't even been out together yet, so booking a holiday might be a bit premature. And anyway, he'd burn, with his ginger-person's skin. As I said this, I was again amazed that I should care about a ginger person – I always go out with dark-skinned brown-eyed men, although looking logically at the past few years, I had to admit it hasn't been an entirely successful policy.

There was Keith for a start, who was mad – very bright on his good days and very very scary on his bad days, and eventually I just couldn't cope any more. He was jealous, and selfish, and I lived with him for so long I thought this was normal. Before him there was Andy, who was an easygoing, lovable light-hearted kind of chap, always well-balanced and cheerful – so much so that I never really knew if he loved me or not. And before him there was dearJon, who was funny and incredibly at ease with himself and dumped me just before my finals. All of them dark-skinned and brown-eyed – like me really. All of them good-looking, all of them men I loved for a long time but was never in love with. Funny I never gave it much thought until then.

Margaret doesn't go for any one physical type, but her men do tend to be married with possessive wives who don't understand their essentially creative natures. I wondered briefly if I should warn her against going out with policemen, but then I wasn't exactly in a position to do so convincingly.

We talked for an hour or so. Margaret changed the CD and put on Tori Amos, we ate more snacks and finally made a bowl of salad to pick at while watching crap telly. To all intents and purposes a pleasant evening – a quiet night in. I felt closer to Margaret than I had done for ages, although I still hadn't told her anything.

Decided not to phone JJ. Thought it best not to talk to him until I'd sorted my head out a bit better. Although I did think I might be getting there – I felt more organised and in control than the last few days. Which was good.

Sunday morning.

I finally decided to be practical and drag out the grey pinstripe skirt and white silk top from the back of my wardrobe. I could almost be packing for a holiday, I thought, laying selected items on the bed. Packing to go away on a long trip to somewhere sunny and exotic, a safari or a trek, running away from home, setting out on an adventure ... Felt a moment of regret for the skirt, which was from a sale at Austin Reed at the start of summer, but, after all, it is only a skirt. Crumpled and still damp from not having been hung out on the line, but clean, in need of a careful iron and a skirt hanger. No such luck, skirt and top both went into a carrier bag along with my favourite flat black shoes. From the Bally sale, last autumn, they fitted beautifully and were made from such lovely soft leather. Getting into the mood, I threw in a pair of horrid yellow tights, biggest mistake of last year, and a thermal top with a gaping hole under one arm, a thin white cotton blouse I never wore, a baggy saggy night-shirt and a pair of black kneehigh leather boots, knotted laces trailing out of the bag. Then I collected the green glass bottles into one bag and the clear glass jars into another, stuffed an armful of papers into the clothes bag and put them all by the front door to be recycled. As I'd have to go to the leisure centre car park to the nearest recycling bins, I thought I might as well go to the gym.

Margaret decided to come too. She was suffering from translator's block, a common event, and felt that deadline or no deadline a workout might help. She carried the paper-and-cloth bag; I took the bottles and jars. Rather more bottles than I could comfortably carry – not that we drank too much, more that we don't recycle often enough.

I hoped.

The car park was empty, as it was still early. Most people who use our gym on Sundays do so as an act of penance after an over-indulgent Saturday night at the pub/restaurant/club. I glanced round as we approached the clothes bin and felt ridiculous. There was a little old lady in an unnecessarily thick coat for the time of year, balanced on her tiptoes, sliding gin bottles one after the other into the bottle-bank. She gave us a conspiratorial smile from under her battered red hat and walked briskly away, no doubt to early mass. Margaret stuffed newspapers into the paperbin, I bundled up the clothing and thrust the bundle into the back of the clothesbin. Wondered whether they would be shredded and recycled or sent off to a disaster victim, and if so, what she'll make of my offerings. Threw the bottles gaily into the bottlebank, relishing the crash as they shattered against the massed glassy contents. Entered the gym feeling cleansed and cheerful, almost chipper, I would say. Sing if you're glad to be green ...

Half an hour on the exercise bike, twenty minutes

on the stepper, twelve on the treadmill and four on the rowing machine. The gym staff had put on a high-energy tape and turned it up and I was really getting into it. Couldn't really be bothered with the weights machines, but bashed out a few token lateral pulldowns and abdominal crunches. Not bad, considering how long it has been since the last time I came in here. I used to go most days when I was in uniform, working shifts, because you could always pop in at odd times when the gym is empty, except for other shift workers or the unemployed – like 0730 hrs, on the way home from nights, or 1530 hrs, after an early turn. Since going on to the robbery squad, the CID course and now the Child Protection Unit, I have to go at normal times, when it tends to be busy with ordinary people. I'm not usually awake and active early on a Sunday, and, of course, I'm much less likely to get into fights these days, so it didn't seem so important to be toned and quick.

Margaret spent most of the time on an exercise bike, pedalling slowly and reading a back issue of *Health and Fitness* magazine with apparent interest. She was wearing a pair of white see-through stripy leggings, showing her floral-patterned lacy Marks and Sparks pants, and a red tie-dyed vest, an unlikely combination in the gym, where most of the women wear matching Nike or Reebok outfits. I was not much better, though, in an old yellow pair of men's swimming trunks and a cropped black Adidas top. Still, the mirrors along the wall reassured me that I may have been neglecting the gym but all that swimming had kept me in reasonable shape. I wondered what JJ will think of what I look like naked? I wished I'd had a better look at him in the bath on Saturday morning.

We didn't bother to shower at the gym, avoiding the too-small changing area with its battered and broken lockers and grey tiled showers, preferring to walk home and change there.

On Sundays we often go for picnics, taking a selection of snacks and drinks and Sunday papers, and this Sunday we opted for Wimbledon Common. It's a short bus ride away and for once the Sunday service didn't let us down. The large black woman driver was loudly humming hymns and Margaret joined in because she can sing in tune and doesn't mind who knows it. The driver started harmonising and was obviously enjoying herself, and Margaret started banging out a rhythm on the back of the seat in front of us. I can't sing – one of my first school memories is of a Christmas concert that everyone's parents were coming to, and being told to stand at the back and mime, so as not to spoil the whole day for everyone else by singing. But I have got rhythm, if I say so myself, and in a couple of minutes we had the whole bus joining in. Even after we'd got off, we could hear singing as the bus ground its way along the side of the common. Margaret got a whole carriage full of drunks singing 'If you're happy and you know it clap your hands' on a south-bound Northern Line train one night last winter, and has plans to get a whole train going one night soon.

We have a regular spot on the common but it had been taken by a loud group of studenty types, pretending to be studying something, all sunglasses and files and fluttering pages, so we ventured further than usual to a more peaceful area. We stretched out on my old pink cotton rug, claiming our six feet of happiness.

The common was dusty and scruffy and full of scurrying families with dogs and kites and bicycles, the contemplation of which helped us enjoy our indolence. We had a lazy afternoon, again, which was great. I felt weary, bone tired, as if I needed to rest and recuperate, as if I'd had an illness or virus or nervous breakdown and must recoup my strength. Whatever was to come in the week ahead, I didn't expect to enjoy all that much of it.

I stretched out in the shade of a sycamore tree, pointing my toes and forcing my arms out as far as they'll go, in an imitation of one of the stretches Cat does in between naps, and breathed as slowly and deeply as I could. There were rooks and squirrels overhead and children shouting in the distance to distract me as I tried to remember all the things I thought I had to sort out during the past week. Candy was still a major worry – she'd take up a large part of each day. I'd hardly be in the office this week. No doubt someone would phone me if there were any major developments.

I'd saved the job pages from several papers this week but I doubted if I would have time to look for another job – and who would pay me to work for them, apart from the police? How would I explain my desire to leave and start again somewhere else? I didn't know what other job I could do, and I didn't feel like starting at the bottom of some huge company or working for nothing to get experience. Maybe I could get a cushy job in security, advising a high-street chain on how to catch shoplifters.

I realised that I seemed to have got through another week without contacting my family, which would be bad, except that now I'd got the excuse of not wanting them to be involved in my affairs. And on the subject of affairs, I thought of JJ again – how we'll act towards each other at work if we meet, how I'll get through the week if we don't meet, whether to phone him or wait for him to phone me. Didn't seem right to worry about things like telephone etiquette, somehow, when I've known him for so long.

I watched a small group of figures in the distance come closer towards us, a woman with a couple of kids and a small black bouncy dog. Normal everyday family getting on with their lives. Wondered what that feels like. Wondered if I'd like it. Then as they approached I saw that the smaller child had ice cream caked all over its face, scabby knees and a bad-tempered whiny voice. It was complaining about something to its mother, who wasn't listening because the dog was having a crap in the middle of the path and she was looking round to see if anyone had noticed or if she could get away with leaving it there, while the larger child had picked up a stick with a few leaves still attached and was trying to poke the smaller one in the eye with it, which provoked an even greater volume of whinge.

Maybe being single isn't such a bad thing, I thought, as Margaret jumped up and grabbed the stick from the larger child and offered it to the mother to flick the dog turd into the bushes.

Wondered why I didn't do that. Decided that I didn't care about people I didn't care about. Made a depressingly short list of the people I do care about. Opened another bottle of beer and reached for the review section of the paper. Which was, as ever, irritatingly full of smug people asserting their superiority by being clever about other people's creations, reports on books and plays I knew I was never going to be interested in, reviews I would skim through. But what was the point? There was never anyone at work to talk to about these things and Margaret knew far more about popular culture than I did – she actually goes to the theatre for fun.

I read a couple of paperback reviews and decided to rejoin the library, start reading again, occupy my mind with made-up crime and horror.

Reminded me of one time I was in the video shop and it was closing and the spotty young assistant with a bad haircut was getting annoyed with my indecisiveness and said, 'Here, have this, it's got excitement, suspense, a great car chase and is this year's best all-round action picture', and I said, 'No, ta, I get quite enough of that at work, thank you.'

So we daydreamed and sunned ourselves in the park, while all around us parents smacked their ugly brattish children, large boys and girls bullied small boys and girls, the madman of the common was doubtless wandering happily around with an axe up his jumper, dodgy-looking blokes were hanging around the play areas watching the children far more closely than the au pairs ever do, animals ate bits of each other, leaving pathetic scraps of fur or feather or bone, and further afield cars drove too fast, people drank too much, they shout and rage and hurt and maim and kill, and when you got into thinking about all that you realised that whatever you personally may have done wasn't really that huge or important in the scale of things and you were falling into the trap of placing yourself in the centre of it all. It was just a matter of remembering the whole picture and not dramatising your own small part in it.

Margaret agreed that the world was a terrible place and there was not much we could do about it. We went home for tea and cake.

And that was Sunday, really.

Dreamed about a woman in a leopardskin catsuit, in a room full of cushions, a scary woman with a mask on, and everything is purple and gold and I didn't like it at all, and she wanted me to do something for her and I was scared of her but wouldn't do it and she was about to be so furious that I woke up frightened.

Investigation: data-gathering

NB: THEFT ACTS, 1968, 1978

The 1968 Act was supposed to cover all possible theft offences and was so good they had to do another one in 1978. My personal favourites are 'obtaining pecuniary advantage by deception' and 'abstracting electricity' – great stuff.

Monday morning was spent in court with Candy and her mother. Candy read her books and played her games and we pretended to ourselves we were just having a day together, although it was obvious from her rushed speech and occasional breath-lessness that Candy knew she would be called through into the child witness room at some stage. I had a pager message at eleven from Steady, letting me know that MacDonald's funeral was to be on Wednesday lunch time in north London. It was expected that there would be a large turnout of serving and former colleagues, and Julie, Steady and I could attend or not, as we saw fit. Steady himself was going, as he had worked with MacDonald and knew his family slightly. I thought about it for about two seconds and decided I would give it a miss.

My second message of the morning, which again buzzed at my waist and made me jump and Candy laugh, was from JJ, asking me to ring the incident room to be formally tasked with visiting the dead man's family to talk to the daughters. Apparently this was to be an informal chat without their mother present, but I could borrow a uniformed PC from King's Cross to do the scribing for me. JJ's message ended, 'love from JJ', which made me smile. Although he probably ends all his messages like that.

I rang the incident room and spoke to a DS Bradwell that I'd never met before and hope never to meet again if he's always that rude.

I said, 'This is DC Barratt. I'm going to be speaking to the daughters of Mr MacDonald, have you any instructions for me?'

He said, 'Well, you seem to know all about it. I take it you are trained for this in some way?'

I said, 'Yes, but I would like to have some sort of official instruction or guideline as to what the expected outcome is, whether it is to be done so as not to miss some remote chance or whether it is seriously expected to bring out any new or relevant information, and I thought that knowing how the investigation in general was going might be a help, and –'

He said, why didn't I do my job and let him get on with doing his?

Well, thanks very much, you've been a joy to speak to, I thought, saying, 'Certainly, Sarge, you can expect my report by Wednesday afternoon at the latest.'

So much for subtly charming some information out of him.

So then I had to arrange to see the girls, which in the spirit of getting-it-over-with I arranged for that night at around seven. Mrs MacDonald was very well spoken and sounded fairly pleasant but not very interested, as if I was pushy to have asked and it was really a bit too much trouble, but she would let me visit none the less. I ended up feeling that she was too well bred to turn me down, but wasn't that keen to see me.

Having dropped Candy and her mother back at their house and wriggled out of fetching the rest of the family from their childminder because Candy's mother thought it would be easier for me to drive round twice to the next street than it would be for her to walk there, I popped into the office en route to the MacDonald house just to see how things were going. I'd hate to miss out on anything.

Julie had left a message on the board to the effect that she was out interviewing someone or other, something to do with one of her jobs she was playing very close to the chest, but Steady was in our office, getting ready to go to the gym round the corner. It was obviously one of his staying-in-town nights. I had a couple of messages stuck to my desk, nothing urgent – a note from Nina to ring her when convenient, and another from JJ saying the same thing. Steady was grumbling about having to go home the following night to fetch a black tie for the funeral, having already promised his girlfriend he'd be staying at her place, and as usual I could not find any sympathy for his troubles at all. He called me a heartless cow, I reminded him he was an ugly cheating sexist git, and we parted on the best of terms as I set off again to meet the family.

DS Andrews rang me to ask for my home phone number, and I said, 'But can't you talk to me now?' and he snorted with laughter at the idea that he might want to talk to me. So that was that. Looked as if Margaret had made an impression the other night.

I called in at King's Cross to borrow a uniformed

constable, as suggested, and was fortunate to get Angela Parkes, a woman I knew slightly from a victim support course we'd both been on a few years back, before I got into CID and got out of the King's Cross office. She's a capable unfussy, slow-moving woman from the East End, loads of common sense and a knack of surprising you by thinking odd thoughts.

We drove through heavy traffic cheerfully enough, exchanging gossip and news about people we hadn't seen or even, in some cases, hadn't thought about for a while. I talked a little about the Candy case and she told me about the sad transvestite who kept coming up to her and asking advice about sex change operations and their availability in other European countries. As Angela said, why do people expect police officers to know everything about everything? Why don't they look it up in the library or ask someone who does know? She told me about a six-year-old kid she'd 'arrested' for brandishing a carving knife in the local post office and demanding money, and I told her the story of the day the year before when I went out early with the robbery squad to arrest a young robber, a six-foot sixteen-year-old who had been very active, using a knife or a broken bottle to threaten other kids and even a couple of adults. Four of us went, one being a dog-handler, expecting a bit of a bundle with him and when we knocked on his door at 0700 hrs one day his mother answered, very bitter to be woken so early, and said, no, we couldn't speak to little Dean because he was still out on his mountain bike doing his paper round.

On our way to the MacDonalds we had the police radio on low and a local music channel on slightly louder, and the traffic wasn't as bad as it often is – at least it kept on moving.

The house was huge, a Victorian semi in warm-looking red brick, glowing behind a trim hedge in a street of similar houses, many of them converted into flats and bedsits with multiple doorbells and several cars in each driveway. The MacDonalds' was one of the better kept in the street, with recently painted door and windowframes and a neat front garden, rosebeds edged with whitepainted stones. Neat porch with stained glass lights and a tiled floor. Three stone steps up to the door. The style of the house was such that a black wreath on the front door and heavily draped windows would not have looked out of place. However, there were no such signs, and as I parked outside and we climbed out of the car I could hear music blaring out of an open upstairs window. There was a television on in the front room, with nobody watching it, and I wondered if anyone inside had heard the faint doorbell above the other noises.

Within a couple of seconds the door was opened by a tiny, exquisitely groomed oriental woman with glossy black hair and flawless skin, barefoot and dressed in flowing black clothes, a very attractive slim woman in her late thirties, I supposed, and I was momentarily at a loss as to what to say or how to say it.

Mrs MacDonald smiled graciously. 'You must be Louisa,' she said, 'and a colleague. I was expecting you both. I'm Lin MacDonald. Come in and meet the girls.'

We followed her down a tiled hall to the large kitchen at the back of the house, where open French windows led out to a pretty garden. There was a teenage girl at a picnic table, finishing off a plate of pasta, and Lin disappeared back into the house to fetch the other sister while we sat at the pine kitchen table and raised our eyebrows at each other.

Angela said quietly, 'You could have warned me. First of all I thought she was the housekeeper or something, then I thought, no, housekeepers can't afford clothes like that. Nobody told me he had a mail-order wife.'

'It's as much of a surprise to me,' I said. 'I had absolutely no idea, either. I suppose I was expecting a middle-aged, mumsy sort of person, with a sour expression and –'

The surprising Mrs MacDonald reappeared with a younger girl, and called in her sister from the garden. 'This is Jenny and this is Kate,' she said. 'And these two ladies are here to talk to you about your father. Why don't you go and chat in the garden, I'll be in the kitchen if you need me. Jenny, you can have something to eat first, while they talk to Kate. That OK?' she asked, leaving little room to argue if it wasn't. I got the impression that Lin MacDonald was very well used to getting what she wanted and Angela and I agreed that we would indeed talk to the older girl first.

We sat round the picnic table in the early evening warmth. Jenny brought us cold drinks carefully on a tray and Angela got out a notebook.

'I'm Louisa and this is Angela,' I said. 'She's going to write down what we say because I've got a terrible memory, OK?'

Kate nodded, looking serious. 'I don't think I can really help,' she said. 'I don't know why anyone would want to kill my dad. I never saw him argue with anyone, I hardly ever saw him at all really. So what do you want to know?'

We went through a few basic questions, about when she last saw him, what mood he was in, what sort of things he liked to do, what upset him, which of his friends and colleagues she had met. The results weren't encouraging from the point of view of forwarding the investigation. She saw her father when it was one of their birthdays, at Christmas, and for a couple of weeks during the summer holidays, except for this year, when she'd chosen to stay with friends instead of coming home from school. Her school turned out to be a very expensive boarding school, also attended by Jenny. The family appeared to spend little time together and Kate seemed almost unmoved by the fact that her father was dead. She couldn't name a single one of his friends or colleagues and wouldn't know if he'd had any unusual calls. She could not remember him ever having had visitors at the house.

Angela dutifully took down the relevant answers but after ten minutes or so I decided to call a halt.

Jenny then came out and told us more or less the same story. She had very little to say about her father. Apparently by the time she was three or four he'd become so busy at work that she never got to know him at all. The two girls and their mother appeared to have formed a close and self-sufficient unit into which MacDonald had rarely intruded.

Both girls were beautiful, articulate, scaled-down versions of their mother, although with brown hair. It was hard to see the influence of gross MacDonald genes in their petite figures and graceful faces.

I would have liked to talk to Lin at greater length, for personal curiosity, but this would have been way off my remit. She seemed unconcerned as to what the girls could have told me – obviously no guilty secrets there – and it seemed that any previous mention of strange goings-on was no more than an attempt to divert attention away from herself and her kids.

Angela and I talked in the car on the way back to King's Cross, where she had a late turn to finish. We didn't hurry back – I was on overtime and she only had a few hours of trundling round the streets on foot patrol giving tourist information to look forward to, moving on drunks and toms and hoping not to get stabbed by a nutter or a druggie.

'Christ,' she said. 'I hope my family care more than that when I go. I reckon that wife must have another bloke in the background. What do you think? She hardly dresses like that for the sake of the girls.'

'I'm just wondering where all the money comes from, and will they miss that now he's dead? I know they'll get his pension, but two girls at boarding school, that huge house ... You have to ask yourself how they do that on a policeman's wages. She doesn't work, so there must be some family wealth or something.'

'Or else he was bent,' supplied Angela. 'That's more likely. I mean, if there was family money, he wouldn't have joined the police, would he? He'd have worked in the city or something.'

I had thought about this myself. MacDonald had been in Vice in London and the Midlands, one of the areas where it is popularly believed that an unscrupulous copper can coin it in. There have been various high profile cases where senior police officers have been suspected of running prostitutes, organising various illegal activities, selling drugs and so on. Not many of them are ever charged with anything, of course, but then, any number take early retirement and get away with things for the good of the job. I mean, think of the public reaction – best they never know, eh? We've got to keep up the public's confidence in the police force or what would happen to law and order? And better that a few policemen line their pockets than all the money going to criminals, surely.

'The only time I ever could have made a bit on the side was on a drugs job,' Angela told me. 'I was told to carry a bag full of dope to the labs for analysis, and when I handed it over I realised that the exhibit label mentioned 'one block of herbal resin' when there were two of them in there. If I'd only checked earlier, I could have made a nice little profit, or had a few good parties.'

'Or been found out and sacked,' I added. 'You know, they were doing that for a while a couple of years ago, testing people out like that until the CPS decided it was *agent provocateur*.'

'Yeah, knowing my luck ... but it could have been worse – imagine if the label had said, 'three blocks of herbal resin'. It made me more careful, I can tell you.'

I dropped Angela off, stopping for a strong cup of black coffee with her in their mess room before returning the car to the yard and writing up my report. All her complaints and stories about the continual petty crime and ignorant people she had to deal with every day reminded me that going back into uniform might not be the answer to my current crisis.

I considered going home but saw a light on in the incident room and went upstairs on the off chance.

JJ was sitting at a desk in the far corner, seemingly immersed in paperwork, but as I entered he looked up and smiled warily at me. 'I see you've been tasked with a family visit, DC Barratt,' he said.

I realised this was to be strictly business, noting how close he sat to another DC's desk. I knew from talking to Nina that there were rumours about our relationship, so all eyes and ears in the room would be on us.

'Been tasked, been visiting, and written up,' I replied. 'Here's the contemp. notes from the MacDonald daughters, not that they'll tell you much.' I dropped my voice to ask, 'Have you got a few minutes to talk? Maybe in the canteen?'

'Well we can't talk in here – but look, here's DS Bradwell,' he added, as the man I'd spoken to at lunch time entered the room.

I'd have recognised him without the introduction, as he was quite the most disagreeable-looking man I'd ever seen (scrappy grey hair on top of a head like you'd see on a Roman coin, on top of a bulky short body) and I've seen, met and interviewed some nasty people in my time. I could only hope he got that expression through years of miserable home life or chronic indigestion. The man barely had the decency to acknowledge my presence; I could, however, sense that he didn't approve of me being there.

I made a show of placing the notes on DS Bradwell's desk and in doing so spotted a photocopy of an interview transcript. It appeared to be a hopeful sort of a usual-suspect-maybe-we'll-get-lucky-here interview by the delightful DS Bradwell. I slipped it inside my jacket to read later at home. Well, I am a detective, you learn to pick up information wherever you can, and it is always useful to read other people's interviews – you can pick up good technical tips.

At the door I paused and turned to wave to JJ, but he was talking to someone on the phone, his pained facial expression suggesting it was not a social call.

Took a train most of the way home – didn't fancy going underground for some reason – and walked the last mile and a half alongside the common. Rang Margaret from the corner and picked up a curry from the Balti house. It's one of those places where you'd rather not eat the meat but the vegetable dansak is just divine, and they do a wicked Bombay potato side dish. I can never work out if the little bloke in the curry house fancies me or whether everyone gets free chutney and poppadoms.

Stuffed face, tidied room, put clothes in machine to wash overnight, drank tea, hot bath, cold beer, retired upstairs to bed to read the bedtime story I'd acquired earlier.

The interview had been done the previous evening with a suspect who was well known to me and indeed probably to most police officers in the area. He'd introduced himself to me years ago as 'Ron the Poet' but I soon learned that 'Ron the Headcase' would be more accurate – he had a list of convictions you could paper a room with and although charming when sober, he was breathtakingly violent when drunk. A vagrant had once complained that Ron had beaten him up, said he wanted to press charges and made a statement, and he was found three days later in a rubbish skip with his throat cut. No witnesses ever came forward and Ron claimed to have been halfway through an almighty bender at the time and had no memory of the day at all, so it never even went to court.

It seemed that in the absence of any clear suspects in the MacDonald case, they'd pulled Ron in on the off chance, as one of the area's most-likely-to-be-involved characters, and you really couldn't fault the logic of it: even if he hadn't done it, he'd probably got away with similar or worse and deserved the hassle. So I had fourteen pages of increasingly pointed and accusatory questioning from DS Bradwell to enjoy, and even though Ron was obviously completely in the dark as to the offence, on suspicion of which he had been arrested, he ended up coughing to an indecent assault on a fifteen-year-old girl in a multi-storey car-park in Guildford on the day, to establish that it couldn't have been him who had done whatever had been done in the alley near the Oceana Fish Bar.

So something good was coming out of the investigation, frustrating though the incident room team understandably found it.

Rang JJ early at work Tuesday. Knew he'd be in before I had even left the house. They make an absolute fortune in overtime on incident room duty, I tell you. He sounded pleased to hear from me, but cagey, as if there was someone else there, or listening in, or he'd been told not to talk to anyone outside the investigation. I asked him the standard question you get on the radio when the person you're checking out is a known nutter – 'Are you free to talk?' And the reply was an emphatic 'Negative, over.'

I mentioned the suspicious thoughts that Angela and I had had after visiting the address of Mrs MacDonald. It seemed that the obvious affluence had already been raised and that a discreet check had revealed no family money on either side, a holiday home in the French alps, and rather more money in the bank than the average DCI made in a lifetime. Mrs MacD was proving less helpful in the pursuit of this line of enquiry than she had been in the matter of letting her daughters speak to me and Angela. In fact her very expensive solicitor was making representations about the unnecessary harassment of a recently bereaved woman who could not possibly be expected to know the ins and outs of her late and practically estranged husband's business affairs.

So there was some sort of attempt being made to investigate, then ... But JJ again mentioned the odd lack of resources and enthusiasm coming from the head of the team, and said that most of them believed that a few of MacDonald's former colleagues in Vice would be busy covering their tracks and shutting down various operations just to be on the safe side. He told me that the usual-suspect line of investigation hadn't seemed very successful but that checks made on the whereabouts of one suspect, Ron the Poet, showed a lack of a substantiated alibi, so he was going to be re-interviewed later in the day.

There were few other developments, except that a second fingertip search of the alleyway had turned up a possible murder weapon; a heavy cylindrical piece of piping that one of the search team had been leaning his bag against had come away from the wall and was currently being looked at by Forensics. Due to the weather, the time lapse and the fact that every dog in central London probably pissed on it now and then, they weren't expecting much of a result. The surface was too rough to take good prints, anyway. But you never know. Then again, getting a print is not always a breakthrough. It can only be helpful if it matches up with a print you already have on file, and even then it wouldn't be exactly conclusive.

Clearly there were other people around in the incident room, and JJ obviously shared a phone line, as it was picked up a couple of times as we talked. Brief chat, then.

Wonder what was wrong with Ron's story about

being elsewhere at the time? Maybe the victim never reported the assault. Maybe he had actually made it up, hoping it wouldn't be checked. Maybe he had been around the area ... maybe he'd stolen MacDonald's wallet ... maybe he'd actually killed him, or just covered the body in rubbish for fun ...

Spent another day in court. Took Candy home, then went back there half an hour later because her mum paged me and needed a hand because 'she's crying again'. This happens – she'll just start shaking and crying and nobody has yet worked out how to stop her once she's started. We've tried hugs and cuddles, short sharp shocks, distraction, bribery, food, ice cream, the lot. Now we just hold her hands until she sobs herself to sleep. This takes hours. She's so small, where does she get the stamina to go on so long? By the time I get home I'm absolutely knackered. I know I could never do anything to hurt another person like that. Couldn't. Just couldn't.

Court and custody duties

NB: SEXUAL OFFENCES ACT 1956, SECTION 5
It is an offence for a man to have unlawful sexual intercourse with a girl under the age of thirteen. This is punishable by life imprisonment, and quite rightly so. You might think, no need for a separate offence because a girl under thirteen can't consent to intercourse, but remember, much of our law is made by (old, male) judges, and apparently even with a six-year-old you'd have to show a lack of consent . . .

Wednesday 23 July, Wodin's day, MacDonald's funeral day. I woke up confused by a dream in which my sister kept banging on the door and shouting outside the window, demanding to be let in at once, at once, do you hear me? but whenever I tried to let her in there was nobody there. I hardly ever see Josie, although we never quite lose touch, because, after all, you never know when you might need a kidney and I'd rather have one of hers than one of Philip's.

Appropriately grey and overcast, a dull heavy day with a strong chance of a big electric storm later and I was feeling tired and anxious.

Steady paged me at lunch time and I met him briefly in the canteen at court – he was in another courtroom, looking after two young boys, one of whom was kidnapped and dragged round cash points by a couple of dopey muggers who were arrested the next day doing the same thing to the other. He'd been to the funeral and couldn't wait to tell me about it.

'Well, we were there dead early. Julie drove us and got us there in no time by one of her funny taxi routes, even had time for a swift half in the local boozer, and we were just parked up waiting out of the way for the previous funeral to finish, and then when they all started to troop past us, well, right at the back in full uniform with all his medals on, who should we see but Ted Doddy, our beloved commander, trundling along behind the family of the bereaved. Of course, when they were all getting into cars and whatnot I called him over and he thought we were apologising for being late. He started to give us a bollocking for letting him down. Turns out that the daft bugger had only gone to the wrong funeral, stood there all the way through thinking, bad show, so few familiar faces here. God only knows what the family made of it, some copper none of them knew turning up and commiserating with them.

'Maybe they thought it was provided by the church,' I suggested, as Steady went on to explain that the old man was so upset by his error that he hadn't felt up to staying for the right funeral, had excused himself to the widow, who was looking good in a dark grey tailored suit, and hurried off back to headquarters.

As for the actual funeral, it had been a bit of an anticlimax, with no wronged women making scenes, absolutely no grief-stricken girlfriends in need of sympathy or a lift home, no suspicious characters in ill-fitting suits with tattoos peeping out at collar or cuff, paying their last respects in traditional gangland style. And apparently the service itself had been extremely short, to the point of hardly mentioning the dead man at all. The family were composed and dignified. Everyone seemed to breathe a collective sigh of relief when it was over, as if glad that they could now get on with their own lives. Bizarre, really. There were no commissioners or deputies present, which was almost unheard-of. Popular belief has it that there are a couple of assistant chief constables whose sole duty consists of attending funerals and looking serious and concerned. Doddy would have been the highest ranked person there.

Steady had heard a few whispers from various mates, though, along the lines that a scandal was brewing in the Midlands, that although it had looked as if he had got out in time, there could well be a movement afoot to make MacDonald a scapegoat for a number of very dodgy activities that the press had got hold of, and thus the lack of official presence at the funeral indicated a backing-off process, at the end of which everyone would say they were never that close, always suspected he wasn't quite right somehow, never did like that man.

Quite how this would affect the investigation into his murder was unclear. Although if this was going on, then it would be very convenient if he should turn out to have been murdered in some scandalous circumstance, perhaps by a pimp or a drug dealer. Still, knowing he was safely buried six feet down was curiously calming and I felt more cheerful than I had been for a long while.

But there was a serious point to this conversation. Steady was telling me that if I could come up with anything damaging through my contacts on the street, any whiff of corruption or scandal or disgrace, I would be in a very good position to get into all sorts of good books, impress all the right people, help keep everyone else smelling of roses while MacDonald took all the flak on his conveniently dead shoulders. And it might even be true, Steady added, which would be a bonus. He hadn't heard anything on the Ron the Poet angle, so I wondered briefly how far they'd got in the second interview, then returned to the matter in hand. Finished my weak coffee and went back to Candy.

Things seemed to be getting more complicated by the day. I was surrounded by people at cross purposes, I felt I was in the crossfire, when I should have been in the clear. There were moments where I wanted to sit down and cry, it's not fair, it's just not fair – it wasn't my fault. If they don't think Ron did it, who do they think did it? They won't be able to just close the case. You can't let the murder of a DCI go unpunished, even if he was a particularly corrupt DCI. Why won't anyone tell me what is going on?

I am tired, and I am weary. I could sleep for a thousand years ...

Rows and ructions in court that afternoon, at the end of which we were told that Candy would no longer be required. The man had changed his mind again – he was no longer saying it never happened, but that he believed that Candy was over sixteen. He was now pleading guilty to unlawful sexual intercourse but continuing to deny rape, kidnap and grievous bodily harm. Well, at least we wouldn't have to spend any more time hanging around.

Candy and I went out to celebrate – she knows that it is not all over and that there is still a chance, though remote, that a random selection of jurors will have turned up a sick collection of lunatics who will believe the man. But we had that end-of-term feeling, anyway, and went round the corner for pizzas and ice creams. I promised Candy's mother I'd bring her home in time for *Eastenders*. We tried to outdo each other in creating odd pizza toppings – my relatively normal goats' cheese and egg was easily beaten by Candy's vegetarian pizza with extra bacon and beef.

So my part in the trial was over and in theory I could now apply for the leave I was due. The unit is in complete disarray – there was no one in overall charge, no sign of a replacement DCI (maybe they thought the job was jinxed: one gone mad, one clubbed down in an alley). I returned the car and popped in to the office in the off chance Julie was working late.

Her coat was still neatly placed over the back of the chair – old CID trick, could mean anything, lots of people always leave a spare jacket in the office in case anyone is checking on the hours they claim at the end of the week – but I suspected that she was still in the building somewhere and I placed my leave request in a prominent position on her desk, then sifted through my paperwork for a few minutes in case she returned.

I came across the note from Nina and remembered I still hadn't called her back. When I phoned she was on a late turn and Custody was quiet for once, so I nipped over the road for a chat. I should have gone home, really, feeling very tired and nervy but for some reason I felt like staying out.

Nina is an excellent Custody sergeant, she has a good style about her, never gets upset, always makes awkward prisoners think they've got something out of her or scored some sort of point when in fact the supposed compromise is exactly what she wanted in the first place. She always looks good too – neat and tidy, nails always manicured and shirts crisply ironed. Never a hair out of place; she wears it up in a bun and can look schoolmistressy or nannyish when it suits her to do so. A lot of the older men love being told what to do by a smartly dressed woman. Nina could make an absolute fortune if she went into business for herself. She says, good looks are all relative and all her relatives are good-looking, so she has to make the effort.

As usual she had a very attractive PC on gaoler duties. I don't know how she manages it but it can't just be down to coincidence. She must be in charge of their rosters. This time it was the handsome PC Foster, beloved of tarts and toms throughout the patch for his fresh-faced innocence and Christian willingness to save their souls rather than arrest them.

Some cynical people mistrust his motives but you only have to talk to the man to realise he's genuine. What's a born-again Christian doing in the police force? Trying to do some good in the world, apparently.

And why not?

PC Foster put the kettle on and did a round of the cells, offering drinks to the occupants. Not many gaolers do that. I accepted a black coffee which made me feel worse.

Nina got straight to the point. 'One of the prostitutes has told PC Foster that she thinks she saw the DCI the evening he died, but she'll only talk to you about it, says she trusts you more than anyone else in the job. She's given him a phone number you can ring before 5 p.m. any day except Saturday.' She passed me a scrap of paper.

I glanced at it and put it into my jacket pocket. I remembered my dad trying to teach me to play poker when I must have been about nine or ten years old, and how he mocked my childish attempts to keep a poker face. Guess he'd be proud of me now. I placed panic, fear and a sense of having forgotten something vitally important to the back of my mind and concentrated hard on an appropriate reply. 'Thanks, Nina, I'll give her a ring tomorrow,' I said. 'I should be able to see her before I go on leave.'

'Leave? Has the case finished with that poor

kid then?'

'Yeah, well nearly. He's more or less admitted all the main points. He's arguing consent but it's hardly a believable defence – they've seen the size of her, nobody in their right mind would think she was over sixteen, so it's really down to the summing-up and let the jury decide now. I think he'll get fifteen to twenty. The DI in charge wants life but I think that's a bit ambitious with a male judge.'

'So, where are you going? Anywhere good? Or are you staying at home?'

'I'm planning a trip with Margaret, as soon as she can finish a bit of work she's doing – could be next week, could be the week after. I've left Julie a request for annual leave. Can't see her refusing really, we've got nothing major on at the moment and I haven't had any leave this year at all.'

'No wonder you look tired. I wasn't going to mention it but you look as if you've been up all night with some man or other . . .'

Nina was definitely fishing here and I wasn't in the mood to gossip, so I just said, 'Yeah, I was, but not anyone you know', and left it at that.

She sensed my lack of enthusiasm for the subject and changed it slightly. 'You'll never guess what's happened with my new man,' she said, checking that PC Foster was out of earshot. 'Well, I'd appreciate it if you kept this to yourself but I expect the story's out by now, thanks to Radio Lampton, but you know my bloke came out for a drink with some of us the other week, well one of the Sex boys recognised him and eventually decided that he'd better tell me – he was only done a couple of years ago for importing tapes from Amsterdam. You know the sort I mean.'

'So what are you telling me? Is it all over, or are you taking popcorn round to his place every night for a private showing?'

'Oh, right, are you the only one with morals all of a sudden? Of course it's all over, I just haven't told him yet. I need to have a good look round his flat and his place in the country first, see if I can get anything good on him. Bastard. I mean, what does he expect, seeing a policewoman? Does he think I'm stupid? What really annoys me is, he was so serious, wanted to settle down, you know, talked about having kids if he met the right person. I just wish I could charge him with wasting police time.'

I commiserated with Nina in her bad luck with men, and we agreed that we were better off single. All men are pigs, but not all pigs are male ... Nina also innocently asked how my friend Margaret was these days, which I assumed to mean there was something going on between Margaret and DS Andrews. I said she was keeping busy.

As I was leaving I took the opportunity to ask about Ron. Nina told me that he had been in Custody at lunch time, interviewed with solicitor present by DS Bradwell between 1430 and 1545, released on bail at 1615 pending further enquiries.

'Basically,' Nina said. 'I get the impression they don't think it was him, but he's shot himself in the foot with his attempt at an alibi on the first occasion. Seems there's not been an offence reported to match the one he's coughed to, so it'd look, well, dodgy to just let him go, and he's got a right bastard of a solicitor, so they're playing it very carefully. D'you know, he rang his brief at home and said, "Hello mate, it's Ron here", and he came straight down, no duty brief waiting time for our Ronny Shakespeare. I mean, there's enough suspicion to hold and question him on, but nowhere near enough to keep him in.'

His name really is Shakespeare — since he came out of prison at the end of a seven-year stretch reduced to four and a half for good behaviour in the early eighties for stabbing his mother with a kitchen knife, and decided to change it by deed poll.

I walked the long way back to my office via Eversholt Street, half-hoping to run into someone I knew on the way. No such luck. I would have to ring Maria tomorrow, and see what she had to say.

No new messages in my office, and Julie's jacket was gone, along with my leave application.

I rang the incident room but JJ had left and I didn't fancy chatting to DS Bradwell, so I just said something vague about checking in again tomorrow. He already thinks I'm an idiot — might as well play along.

Margaret was out, no note left, Cat claiming to be on the verge of collapse due to lack of food. I picked it up and found it particularly heavy, so it was clearly lying. I found a bowl of Margaret-food in the kitchen, microwaved it and ate it in front of the television. Margaret-food is immediately recognisable, as it consists of large quantities of vegetables hacked into pieces and fried with chickpeas and chillies. Sometimes there's garlic and coriander in there, sometimes not. Today's was the spicy version. I shouldn't talk, really, I only cook two things, soup and curry, the one being a runnier version of the other. It's just laziness – we're both pretty good at party food and special occasion cakes and so on.

I still haven't got round to sitting down and working out how I feel about what I've done. Being quite so tired tonight, it has been looming in on me – I can't keep up the oh-not-now-I'm-busy attitude I've managed to maintain these last eight days or so. So it has been back to the first trick I tried, the getting-it-all-down-on-paper-so-as-not-to-have-to-think-about-it-again approach.

I think about the pages I've written, never printed, sitting silent and safe in my computer; then I think, Margaret uses it sometimes. She isn't very competent, but then again, she might well decide to see what I've been up to these past evenings and odd moments, maybe trying to be helpful, see if there's anything she can do, tidy up the desktop, or give me a few handy hints on achieving a more professional style and presentation.

'Catch yerself on,' I say aloud. 'Get a grip, this is too stupid.' I'm just frightening myself, un-necessarily. I decide to get a couple of things done before facing up to a couple of other things, quite rationally, and until such time as I feel better about life in general I'm in no state to dwell on morbid and unpleasant events I certainly can't change now. I remind myself that whatever you do is done be-cause at the time it is the best thing that you can do.

Hot bath, cold beer or three. Wish I knew how much to drink to sleep without dreams and wake without a headache. Shouldn't be too much to ask, surely.

I dream that I am in a train, underground al-though not an Underground train, nor is it the Eurostar. It is old and possibly a mining train or a tourist train, as we are going quite slowly through caverns and caves that appear to be mainly natural but with some evidence of rock blasting here and there. The roof is low at times and I could reach up and touch the rough stone surface which would be cold and damp. I can't see the front or back of the train but I know it is long, stretching a long way in front and behind me. There are hundreds of people on this train but they are all silent; the only sound is the train itself rumbling and clattering along, a sound that echoes back from, yet seems muffled by, the low ceiling and rough walls.

After a short while the train slows down and stops and there is a murmur of conversation as people wonder what is going on. Nobody has any instructions and there doesn't seem to be anyone in charge. I realise that this is my stop and I get off, climbing down from the carriage and then watching with regret as the train slowly moves away without me. The cave here is enormous, fading into darkness at the edges, so its exact size is unclear. The rough floor surface has been smoothed over into a semblance of a station platform. The air is cold and there is no breeze, not even the air-rushing-through tunnels you get on the tube. I turn to the man on the platform, who comes up to me with a clipboard in his hand. He is young, with a pale pointy face, dressed in black, and there is something art-studenty about his appearance, with his short cropped red hair and triangular goatee beard. I know he is the devil, and he knows me too.

He shakes my hand and we sit together on a bench hewn in the rock wall. He shows me the clipboard, on which he has been drawing cartoons, and the picures and words don't quite make sense. It is as if the words are in a foreign language and so in some way are the drawings. He is saddened that I can't see the joke. Then he frowns and flips over a few pages, coming to a printed page which he scans closely. Then he smiles at me again, this time with great sadness, and shakes his neat head.

'But you're early,' he says. 'I'm sorry but you'll have to go back. Look,' he insists, showing me a name and date, 'you see?'

The train comes past again and I get on, already almost waking up , desperately trying to remember the date on the page with my name, but I can hear faint faraway laughter and understand that I won't ever remember the date. It is not allowed.

I think about this for a while when I wake up. I've always had vivid dreams, often in colour and usually involving people I know. This particular one was odd but I feel strangely pleased with it, almost as if I have been pardoned or at least given a reprieve for something.

Wish I could remember the date on the paper, though. I could tell a few people and then if anything odd happened on that date, they would be well impressed.

Further witness statement

NB: THEFT ACT, 1968, SECTION 21
Backmail used to be money paid to Scottish people to stop them attacking you – the man in the street might think it still is – now, however, it is defined as being, the making of unwarranted demands with menaces. There is room to argue what exactly constitutes menaces, and whether a demand is warranted on a particular occasion.

OK, so I had to see Maria. How do people generally

do things they'd really rather not? I suppose if you are religious or properly brought up, you have a sense of duty to see you through those awkward times, or a sense of guilt that forces you into action. I've always hoped to avoid duty and guilt as much as possible. And in this particular case neither would have been much help. But I hate having things hanging over me. I try and get unpleasant things out of the way as soon as I can. Except going to the dentist, I can put that off for years. Generally, I worry, although I have managed to develop a range of distraction techniques to keep the worries under control.

Today I went in to work early, rang Maria at 0830 hrs, and was round at her mother's flat by 0915 hrs. This was on the third floor of a six-storey block, a long building with external staircases decorated with graffiti and littered with papers and bottles and empty cans. There were lifts, but I knew it would be pointless to try the button, there was no chance it would actually work. And I'd have to wash my hands if I touched it. Stairs were probably safer, anyway. Each floor had a low wall running round the outside and the front doors were painted in different primary colours in an effort to cheer the place up, although you had to be there to spot this because most of them were protected by heavy mesh outer doors in grey or black steel.

The lovely Maria was in and was sober for once, which was a bit of a bonus.

'I hear you want to talk to me,' I started off as soon as we were settled at the kitchen table with a mug of tea.

I've been in plenty of houses at work where I wouldn't want to drink anything, flats where you don't want to sit down for fear of sticking to the settee, places with babies' nappies and used syringes and fresh dog turds on the floor, rotting food on the table and filthy children crawling from one potentially lethal plaything to another, but Maria's mother turned out to be one of those brilliant middle-aged neurotics who spend all day scouring and cleaning, who love the smell of bleach and wear rubber gloves for seventy-five per cent of their waking lives. The flat was therefore spotlessly clean with a refreshing smell of pine disinfectant. Wish I had a housemate like that ... The room was cosy if a bit too warm, not a mote of dust anywhere, with lace covers on the chairbacks. No doubt there was a spare roll of loo paper under a Spanish doll in the bathroom.

Maria looked at me across the squeaky-clean formica table top. She looked terrible, dark ringed eyes, traces of make-up in their corners and a fading yellow bruise on the side of her forehead. But then, she had only just finished work. 'Yeah,' she said, looking away again, seeking something else to focus on and finding only scrubbed surfaces and polished flooring, eventually settling for staring into her tea.

I sighed. This wasn't exactly easy. I'd rather have

been almost anywhere else, doing most other activities imaginable, but here I was in the kitchen of a retired prostitute trying to persuade a tired prostitute to tell me that she'd seen me talking to someone a few minutes before he was brutally killed. How's that for a scenario for training school, I thought, what is the correct interview technique in these circumstances? Put her at ease, build up a rapport, convince her that she wants to talk to you, be sympathetic, nod, smile, use non-verbal encouragements, use silence ...

'Listen, Maria, I'm really busy today and I'm sure you need some sleep. So come on, what's the matter?'

Maria looked around again. 'Oh, you may as well know,' she said slowly. 'D'you remember the last time I talked to you? When I was with Alison, and there was this bloke who came up to us?'

'Yes, I remember,' I said. 'What about him, is there something we should know?'

It amazes me sometimes when I'm talking to people, usually in interview, and they start to tell me things, how detached I can get from what they are saying. You get so concentrated on getting as much from them as they can possibly provide, that the content becomes irrelevant, the story is all-important, whether it's a twelve-year-old boy explaining why he suffocated his friend's granny, or a 45-year-old man telling you how his ten-year-old neighbour was always giving him the eye and showing him her knickers, somehow you don't judge or comment, you just keep on asking for more details as if it's the most natural conversation in the world, as if you understand. Or you can't quite understand, but if they could just fill in a few more details or explain that last bit one more time ... So here I was talking to Maria as if I knew nothing and she could help us with our enquiries.

'Alison said he reminded her of someone who was bad news,' said Maria, rushing it out now that she had finally gathered the words together, 'and I agreed, but when I asked that nice PC Foster about it, when we knew he'd been killed, that bloke, and he told me his name and I started to think about it a bit more in case I could help ...' She almost blushed.

She caught my eye, looking to see if I'd noticed that she was trying to help the nice policeman because she fancied him, and I smiled and said, 'go on.'

'Well, then I realised I did know him, but from years ago. He had black hair and was thinner then but I'm sure it was him. I know he was a policeman and I think he worked in Soho. Maybe Vine Street Station.' She paused and looked to me for confirmation and I nodded. 'Anyway, you can believe me or not but I swear on my mother's grave – well, you know what I mean – he was taking money off me and some of the girls and if ever we didn't have any he'd get really violent. He didn't care where he hit you and he raped a friend of mine.'

'Are you sure about this?' I asked cautiously. 'And are you prepared to make an official statement, because if you do, you could be called to coroner's court to give evidence.'

'Oh I'm sure all right,' she answered, and there was the nearest I'd ever heard to real anger in her voice. 'The girl he raped died two years ago, drugs and pneumonia I think it was, so I know that won't be any use, but I swear the rest is true and I'll say it in court if you want me to. I know it's like speaking ill of the dead but he'd have killed me if I spoke out before. There's too many coppers think they can get away with murder, and some of them actually do, for years.'

I decided to ask a further question. 'So was that the last time you saw him, then, the night you were with Alison?'

'Yeah, thank God, he went off towards the Euston Road and I never saw him after that. Well, I wasn't around much later on because just after I was talking to you I happened to get invited to a party in town, so, I wouldn't have seen him, anyway.'

'Oh, right. OK ... this may seem like an odd question,' I said, 'but do you know a chap called Ron, drinks on the street, lives in the estate, has a small yappy dog?'

'Ron the Poet, you mean? Yeah, I know him all right, his dog bit my mum on the leg and she said she'd get it put down. He said he'd burn her out of her flat if she tried. Why d'you want to know?'

'Well there's a suspicion he might have been around the area that night when Mr MacDonald got killed.'

'Well, I definitely saw him that morning, outside the bookies. I think he'd struck it lucky 'cos he had a big bag of beer cans in his hand.'

'Can you remember what time that would have been?' I said, warming to this interview at last.

'Dunno really, maybe around midday.'

At this point I phoned the incident room and talked briefly to JJ, who passed me on to the DS as soon as I told him what Maria had to say.

'That's a tricky one,' he mused. 'I think we'd better stick to the bare minimum for now, until we see which way the bosses are going to play this one.' He paused to think. 'Tell you what, why don't you go for the, um, I recognised the man who I knew from his time at Vine Street, he appeared healthy and was last seen walking towards Euston Road. Mention running into Ron too. How did you know we were on to him by the way? And then we can get her questioned in court for the rest of it if it turns out to be necessary.'

I got out my folder of papers and Maria and I got down to working out a statement that would leave her satisfied that she had told her story, yet leave the exact nature of her previous encounters with Fraser MacDonald unspecified. Not easy at all. I made sure that I explained all the usual stuff about only saying things you know from your own experience, not giving hearsay evidence and not giving a statement on behalf of someone else who would be able to speak for themselves. She seemed to get the message. I don't like taking a statement to order, so to speak, getting someone to say what I want them to say rather than what they intended to say, but I can't say I minded on this occasion.

Statement of MARIA JOANNE SPENCER
Age OVER 21
Occupation (Er, let me see, customer relations? No, can you put unemployed? OK.)
UNEMPLOYED
This statement consisting of ———— pages each signed by me is true to the best of my knowledge and belief and I make it knowing that if tendered in evidence I shall be liable to prosecution if I have wilfully stated anything which I know to be false or do not believe to be true.

On Tuesday 15 July 1997 I was around the King's Cross area for most of the day. I live in the area and generally spend most of my time out and about. At around midday – I know the time because I'd just come out of the hairdressers and my appointment was at 11.00 a.m. – I saw a man called Ron the Poet outside the bookies on Pentonville Road, talking to a young white man I don't know who was begging there. I don't know Ron's surname but I've known him by sight for a few years, he lives in the next block to my mum. Later in the afternoon I met up with a friend and had a drink in the Hart and Dragon. I had two pints of beer but I was not drunk. We left there around 4.00 p.m. and at about 5.30 p.m. I saw a man walking towards me along Eversholt Street. He spoke to me, asking me if I was working that afternoon, and I think he recognised me but he did not say that he did. I recognised this man as being a policeman I first knew five or six years ago. I know this man as Fraser MacDonald and when I knew him he worked out of Vine Street police station. I first met him in the summer of 1991 after an argument in the street with a man who had accused me of stealing money from him, and on this occasion I was arrested by Mr MacDonald and searched by him. He took some money from me that belonged to me and I was then told I was no longer under arrest. The man did not wish any involvement with the police, and as far as I was concerned that was the end of the matter. I wanted to complain about the way Mr MacDonald searched me and pushed me around but he told me it would be easier in the long run if I put up with it because everyone else did the same and nobody would believe me. However, from then on, whenever I saw Mr MacDonald he would demand money from me, threatening to arrest me for being a common prostitute if I did not pay him. I did not report this to the police at the time because I was afraid of him and I knew he was a policeman so it would only lead to trouble. I thought it was best not to annoy him. I estimate that between the summer of 1991 and the following winter I must have met him every couple of weeks and he always took money from me, frequently threatening to beat me or cut my face if I did not do as he said. On one occasion I was arrested for being drunk and taken to Vine Street where I was released without charge after he intervened. I know this will be documented at Vine Street because I saw my custody record there. This was in late 1993, I think November or December. After this occasion he thought that I owed him. He used to say that I owed him one and he'd tell me when I had to pay him back. As time went on he became even more threatening towards me until I began to avoid the area altogether and in the end I moved away and did not see him for three or four years.

The only time I have seen him since then is the evening I have mentioned. I recognised him by his face, build and the way he walked.

I have no doubt that he is the same man. At the time I saw him he appeared to be in good health and had no visible injuries. He was wearing a dark-coloured suit and I think he may have been carrying a black briefcase. I think he may have been slightly drunk because he was swaying a bit as he walked.

When I heard that he had been killed I thought about where I last saw him and I am sure he was walking towards the post office. He was by himself and I did not see anyone else speak to him. I would say the time when he went round the corner and out of sight would have been about 5.32 p.m.

Maria was reasonably happy with this statement, and I explained it would form part of the evidence that was being collected from many different sources, that she might be called to court but might not. I thanked her for coming forward and she smiled.

'I would have made the statement to that PC Foster,' she said, 'but I didn't want him to know how long I've been doing this. I didn't want to have to tell him all the sordid details, you know. I'm not ashamed of how I earn my living, but not everyone can understand that. Hey, I meant to ask earlier, do you think it was Ron, though? There's an awful lot of people round here would love to see him go down for it, d'you know what I mean? Do you want me to see if anyone else saw him around at the right time?'

I gathered up my papers and moved towards the door. 'Only if they really did, Maria,' I replied. 'Perjury is viewed as a serious offence.'

'One thing, though,' said Maria, yawning and rubbing the smears of black eyeliner further across her face. 'You know Alison made a statement? She wants to withdraw it now – she's moving to Manchester with some old boyfriend, her kid's dad, he is. They're playing happy families now he's out of Belmarsh and she doesn't want to have to come back here for court.'

Smart, I thought.

'OK, tell her to trust me. I'll sort it so she won't get called,' I said, pulling the door firmly closed behind me and setting off down the staircase to street level.

Back to work with a lighter step.

I dropped the statement in at the incident room, giving it to DS Bradwell, who skimmed through the contents and tossed it aside without comment. I waved across the room to JJ, who smiled and looked suddenly like the devil in my dream, wearing a black polo neck. He held up his fore-fingers in the T sign and I gave him a thumbs-up in return.

Two minutes later we were comfortably installed at a table in the far corner of the canteen.

Not the most obviously romantic of locations, but it would do for me. I was so pleased to have JJ to myself that I just sat there and smiled at him, taking in his beautiful freckled face and crisply ironed shirt. He was looking concerned and serious but I knew from his eyes that he'd rather be in a more intimate encounter than was advisable in such a public place. If we had so much as sat close together or held hands the news would have been flying round the area within minutes. Might as well take out an advert in the *Police Review*.

But JJ was serious for a reason; he took a deep breath and asked me how I had got on with the statement from Maria. I said, fine, she didn't have much to say that we didn't know or suspect already. Basically, she'd recognised him from years ago and hadn't seen what happened to him or mentioned anyone else as being in the area.

JJ relaxed a little, stretched his shoulders back, shook his head slowly and smiled. 'I'm on your side, you know. I wish you'd trust me ... be careful, Lou,' he continued, 'just be careful ...', and might have explained himself further, had Steady not ambled into the room and given me a wave from the counter.

'There you are,' he said, settling in next to me with an unfeasibly large rock cake, 'I had a message from the CPS for you. They expect a verdict from the Candy case today, although they'll probably delay sentencing for reports. Hey, what were you two so deep in conversation about anyway?'

I explained that I was telling JJ about my dreams,

adding, 'And you were in one of my dreams this week too.'

Steady beamed with pleasure. 'Oh yeah?' he said. 'Good, was I? One of those exotic, erotic, really fantastic sex-on-a-beach dreams?'

I told him he had merely appeared as a helpful signpost in an otherwise bewildering dream, and that it was the first time I could ever remember being pleased to see him. He supposed that that was better than nothing, although he did say that in the next dream he'd rather have a more active role.

By the time he sloped away to visit some woman or other, JJ had to go back to the incident room.

'Come round tonight for dinner,' I invited. 'I'll make something, round about eight?'

'OK, see you later.' And he was off, shouldering the door open and striding away down the corridor. A very physical sort of man. Interesting thought there, but since I was at work I postponed that line of daydream and got myself together, returning to my office to see what needed to be done there.

Julie was in and had signed my leave application, even though I had filled in the dates in pencil.

'I really don't mind when you go,' she explained, 'seeing as there's a review under way and it looks as if we may be about to be merged with the Sex unit, at least for a trial period. The whole department is in chaos and until there's news of an appointment to cover MacDonald, nobody can get anything done. Vic Nolan can't bear to retire while he's nominally in charge but he'd go like a shot if it was sorted, and basically you could probably just not come in to work for a month or two and I doubt if anyone would notice.'

I asked if she'd heard the DC Hadley story, and she hadn't . . .

'Well, JJ was telling me that, over the last three years Hadley was doing a law degree at South Bank University, full time, and the rest of the robbery squad covered for him. He used to go out with them for their early arrests and worked the odd Saturday and nobody ever queried his hours. He's just got his results, passed it, handed in his notice, buggered off on annual leave and we'll probably never see him again.'

Julie agreed that this was an excellent plan, but harder to pull off now that the story had got out.

I skimmed through the collection of papers in my tray – mainly old LIO reports and *Police Gazettes* that everyone else had finished with and couldn't be bothered to file. Missing persons, escapees from prison, stolen goods and unidentified bodies. Fascinating stuff, but unlikely to have anything to do with me. I gathered up a pile of them and dumped them in Steady's tray. Paperwork cleared. I've never known this office so quiet.

Just then, of course, the phone rang and it was one of the uniform PCs calling from the local hospital. There was a kid in there with various things pushed into the back of his eyelids and accident and emergency staff wanted police and social services informed, so they'd grabbed the nearest copper, who happened to be going off duty, and it wasn't really my job but could I pop down and find out what was going on so that he could go home?

So down I went and found a kid who was missing from a home in Sussex, a bright and charming kid who happened to love attention, particularly medical attention, and had spent the train journey up to London stuffing staples out of a magazine into the back of his eyelids because he knew from experience that they'd have to give him a general anaesthetic to get them out, and he was particularly fond of being put under. He'd also opened an old cut, pushed a five pence piece inside and let it close over again. He told me this proudly and I passed it on to the nurse who had seen it all before and sensibly treated the kid with a startling lack of gentleness or civility. I approved of this course of action and showed no concern myself – encourage the boy and he'd be back twice a week, forever looking for more sympathy – and as soon as a social worker turned up from the boy's supposedly secure home, I left him to her.

Found Julie back in the office looking more pre-occupied than usual. She didn't speak.

'What's up?' I asked eventually.

'I've passed my Inspector's Board,' she replied gloomily, 'and they say they'll promote me within the next couple of months. Apparently they want a female inspector to star in the new recruitment brochure – makes you sick, doesn't it? Only good thing I can think of right now is that they'll have to install a senior ladies' beside the senior gents' on the top floor at area headquarters. Anyway, they're hinting at giving me a comfy job at the divisional training school for the rest of the decade.'

'Well, you don't have to apply for it just because you've passed your Board,' I said, trying to cheer her up. 'You could always put in for the area inspector, do a couple of years in uniform and come back to save us all as DI after that.'

'Yeah maybe ...' She refused to be comforted, declined my suggestion of a small celebration and stomped off home still scowling.

Well, that took up most of the afternoon and since I couldn't find anything useful to do, I left ever so slightly early to go home via a supermarket, with cooking a meal for JJ on my mind.

Wild rice, mushroom and red pepper goulash, various bits for a green salad, several extra bottles of beer in the fridge; the preparations were all done by about seven o'clock.

Margaret came in, starving after a long swim and workout at the gym, undertaken in celebration of finishing a poem sequence she'd claimed to have completed and posted a week ago. I explained that I had planned a romantic meal and she was enthusiastic, offering to lay the table and make the salad. I had a quick bath, wondered about putting on my lucky lilac underwear, decided I didn't need it, opted for the casual, didn't-dress-up look. Mainly due to not having any smart clothes; partly due to knowing JJ too long. I mean, he'd seen me red in the face and covered in mud after a two-mile cross-country run at training school, he'd seen me in severe black dress with my hair in a bun at court, he'd seen me throwing up at our passout parade and acting stupidly at numerous social drinks at work since then, so there didn't seem to be much point in trying to impress him now.

Social skills

NB: OFFENCES AGAINST THE PERSON ACT 1861,
SECTIONS 23, 24
*Poisoning people is wrong, more so if you want to
kill them or seriously damage them.*

JJ arrived fashionably late, just as Margaret and I
were finishing off the last of the bottled beer. She
was telling me about a new restaurant she'd been to
and I was just about to find out who she'd been
there with when JJ rang the doorbell. He had turned

up in what I recognised immediately as a job car (spot the extra aerial and check out the filthy bodywork), which was clearly not good news. Either he was still on duty, or he was off duty but anticipated a very very early start in the morning, neither of which left much scope for the sort of getting-to-know-each-other that I had planned for the evening.

He draped himself elegantly over the arm of Cat's chair, and seemed oblivious to the tabby fur settling onto his suit. I thought he'd rather not be told and so said nothing.

Turned out he was both still on duty and ex-pecting an early start – could it be they had a breakthrough in the case? Also turned out that Ron had done a runner, vanished, and elevated himself to the status of prime suspect at the same time. He'd been bailed on condition that he signed on every day at the front desk, and he simply hadn't both-ered. The late turn skipper had sent a couple of probationary PCs round to his flat to arrest him on breach of bail conditions, more for them to gain experience than for any other reason, and they had arrived at the same time as the fire brigade. The flat was gutted, having been quietly smouldering for hours. Charred lumps in what had been the living room were probably the remains of his mongrel dog: Forensics would confirm that. None of the immediate neighbours had reported it until the fire had threatened to spread in their direction. There was no sign of Ron himself; nobody could remember seeing him that day and suddenly it was all go in the incident room, checking last known addresses and hunting up former known associates.

'It is really weird to suddenly abandon all the other possibilities and go for him now,' JJ complained. 'We were getting a lot of stuff through on corruption – there was more than a hint that MacDonald was into drugs and money-laundering in a big way. He had some very unsavoury associates and there was loads still to do. We've not had anywhere near enough support from the word go, we've had no assistance from anyone, they've tried to ban overtime which is never done on an incident room like this, and now they've decided to go all out for someone who's only ever been a very loose suspect. We're nowhere near an answer yet, and I don't believe we'll ever get to find out what really happened.'

'So what's the current theory?' I asked, opening the last beer for myself, since JJ was driving and Margaret was tactfully clattering around upstairs. 'Did he fall or was he pushed?'

'What, MacD? Not much doubt that he was pushed, Lou,' JJ said. 'I reckon his seedy past caught up with him, and nobody seems to want to know any more than that. There's definitely something funny going on – we've done all the usual enquiries, house to house, questioned everyone seen around at the relevant time or arrested on the patch later or likely to have been in the area that night, but it's as if we're trying not to discover anything. You know, I've even caught myself doing it, asking people, I don't suppose you saw anything, I expect you walked the other way that evening, and I don't know why. The only thing that needed following up was that statement – you know the one. Don't suppose you want to fill me in at all?' He gave me one of his looks before he added, 'Thought not.'

'Least said, soonest mended,' I said firmly. 'In any case they want it all kept quiet and swept under the carpet for fear of what might be found out. I mean, I'm not even supposed to be involved in the investigation and I've been told all sorts of stories about the man. I dread to think what the full story might be.'

'Well, it looks as if they've decided to go for Ron. I think DS Bradwell wants to solve this one so he can go for his Inspector's Board with a cleared murder to his name, but there's still been practically no media interest, so someone must be pulling away at some strings somewhere along the line ...' JJ's attention wandered and he stretched his arms out, collecting several thousand extra Cat hairs as he did so. 'Go on,' he said, 'roll out the dinner. I'm starving and I have to get back by nine or the boys will think we've been ... well, you know, um.'

'Tell you what,' I suggested, 'I won't deny anything you say happened, if you don't deny anything I say happened.'

'Thanks but no thanks – I know what you're like when your imagination takes off,' JJ said. 'No, let's just stick to having some dinner with you and your lovely housemate.'

The food seemed to be acceptable – he ate it, anyway – which was, gratifying, I suppose, but after he'd gone back to the office I felt decidedly unsatisfied. At least I got a hug on the doorstep before he went – a proper, body-long hug that felt just right, with no bones or buckles in the way. For six seconds I felt safe and protected, as if his arms reached round me twice, and I almost relaxed for the first time in recent memory. Almost.

Balanced summary of evidence

NB: PUBLIC ORDER ACT 1986, SECTION 2 (4)
Behave respectably at all times and you won't get into trouble.

I guess deep down I wasn't sure why I wanted him, what I wanted from him. I mean, nice guy and all that, great body, good friend, but a ginger? Not that it really mattered, but thinking ahead, what if we did get together, what if we had a kid, what if it was ginger, how would I be able to love it?

I voiced these fears to Margaret, who felt that chances were, maternal instinct could probably overcome even that sort of obstacle. Although we did agree that those fat, red-faced, ginger babies with orange hair plastered across their heads and some sort of skin disease caused by exposure to sunlight would try even the best of parents '... which, let's face it, you wouldn't be,' she pointed out. 'Remember when we were looking after the stray kitten that Cat found, and you wouldn't clear up its mess? And you know how useless you are around people being sick.'

So that left the JJ question still undecided.

Having unexpectedly found myself with an empty evening, no entertainment of any variety planned or available, I decided to finally think things through. I felt strong enough and sorted enough to face up to one or two unpleasantnesses that needed attention.

This time to myself is difficult to deal with. You know how blokes tend to fall apart when they get out of the army? Can't cope with having to take all those minor decisions themselves about how to fill their leisure hours – having leisure hours, even. I've been occupying my mind with day-to-day details so well that it is a shock to suddenly not have something urgent to get on with. What do people usually do between having dinner and going to bed? Margaret has work to do, dictionaries to flip through, sheets of manuscripts to fan out and scowl over, and someone to phone now and then. JJ works overtime in the incident room. Cat has visits to make, titbits to scrounge, doors to scratch and presumably other small furry animals to avoid or sidle up to.

Lists are generally helpful for this kind of thing. I started with Good Things and Bad Things.

GOOD THINGS	BAD THINGS
house	Mr MacDonald
Cat	work
Margaret	
JJ	
holiday	
savings account	

Well, that was encouraging – a clear victory for Good Things by the substantial margin of six to two.

My savings account usually cheers me up – I don't go out much, I travel by public transport, bought the house when prices were low and got a fixed-rate mortgage. When I started saving up it was to buy a camper van, preferably a done-up vintage VW one, pack it full of stuff and go travelling. Then I thought that, maybe I'd get a convertible Beetle or a Karmann Ghia instead, then perhaps a bigger house, or move out into the country. (What would I do in the country?) The savings account is still sitting there awaiting a final decision. Ready and easily accessible, should it be required for saving myself with.

So that is one Very Good Thing.

However, JJ isn't necessarily even a Good Thing. Wondered briefly why it took me so long to think of him, why we didn't get together months ago, why I only discovered I fancied him when it was too late really, after I'd done what I did. Things would have probably worked out differently if we'd started things any other time, but when I was still in protective mode, I was scared, and that's just not true any more. I'm not scared, I'm not helpless and I don't want to be rescued. So what could a knight in shining armour do for me?

The real problem with JJ isn't his hair colour, of course. It is that I don't know how he would feel about me if he knew what had happened the other day with Mr MacDonald. Well, I suppose I hope that he would be reasonable, weigh up the evidence, take into account my character, the mitigating circumstances, look at the self-defence argument and then, if necessary, balance the fact of an unpleasant man being dead against the fact of me being around, see which he thinks is more important, of more value.

More important, more valuable, according to which guidelines exactly? It all depends. We impose values, we don't find them ready made. I think I've sorted mine out.

Of course, you can't do that really, not if you're a policeman. You have to say, there is sufficient evidence to support a prosecution. If there is. Does he actually have to know? Given that it would all be based on a confession, would there still be enough evidence after this amount of time? The clothes I wore are destroyed, there are no witnesses, no forensic evidence, so far as I know, and everyone's aware I've been under stress with Candy. Let's face it, arresting me would hardly be in the public interest.

I can't keep this in focus for very long. What if I don't tell him? How would he find out? He must know or suspect something. He's seen the statement from Alison -- pity I didn't get in there quickly enough to take that one myself, I'm sure I could have sorted it out.

I know that I deserve to walk unmolested in the city where I live.

I know that I have the right to defend myself against attack.

I know that killing someone doesn't make me a worse person than I was before.

But I know that it has made me a different person.

I don't exactly want to be pardoned or forgiven; I don't want to forget and move on.

What do I want, and how can I get it?

I want someone to say they understand. I want someone to know, so that I'm not the only one who knows.

I don't want to be interviewed and cross-examined and brought to trial; I don't want every-one to know, to be an object of common discussion. I don't want the *Sun* talking to my ex-boyfriends. Can you imagine? Would they find them all? What would JJ think if they were lined up and listed? The tabloid headlines, the self-righteous indignation they'd muster. I don't want the general public wondering if I really did it, had MacDonald and I been having a secret affair; why I was in the alley-way with him? Any of that. I could not bear it.

I don't want to go on working with sick and damaged people. I don't care if I never catch an-other robber or squeeze another confession out of a child molester or rapist. I just can't do it any more. I know some officers do it for years, and all I can say is, they must be stronger than me. There's a line from a Nick Drake song that I can't keep out of my head at the moment – 'Time has told me you'll rarely find troubled cure for a troubled mind' – and it feels like a sort of shorthand for how I feel about a lot of things. Maybe I should have sorted myself out a bit better before I joined the police; all the stress and hassle I've volunteered for and chosen for myself hasn't helped me at all. Why did they let me in when I was so clearly a bit mixed up and confused?

I really do need to take that holiday now. To walk away from it all. *Walk*, as they say in police circles. 'How did you get on in court? Did you win?' 'Na, he walked ...'.

They may manage to pin it on Ron the Poet, if they ever catch up with him. My guess is, he'll stay disappeared for a while. Or else turn up dead somewhere, months down the line, and that'll be called a clear-up. 'Cleared by other means', as the phrase has it – police will not be seeking anyone else in connection with this offence.

I think of all the things I have thought, through and through, over the past ten days and I wonder whether they would make sense to anyone else, and what that sense might be. I think of the portrait of Dorian Gray, withering into horrid aged ugliness in a closed room, while the original danced beautifully in the world outside and I wonder about how that could happen. And I face the fact that if I went back to the start, I could easily find that the statement I have made, the story I have told myself, my version of events, bears little resemblance to reality ... that it is altering all the time, that maybe I meant to kill someone all along. Maybe I've been going to the gym and keeping fit all these years so as to be ready for my chance. Maybe I always had a plan and I've been waiting for my opportunity all this time. Maybe nothing has ever felt so good as those last few blows when I knew that I had done enough to defend myself. Maybe I want to move on now because I have had my revenge – I don't need to be in the force any more, some cathartic process has freed me and I can regain some sort of control now, put myself together and vanish.

But you could say that leaving now would be running out on Candy. Abandoning her, leaving her to fester along with the rest of her family. I'd rather look at it in a more positive way. I've set myself up as a role model for her and if I'm getting out, going off to save myself, I'm also showing her it is possible to escape, at least temporarily. And in a way I did what I did because of her, for her and others like her, as well as for myself. So it's not really a betrayal. I'll send her postcards, hopefully interest her in the outside world in all its weirdness and wonderfulness. Show her or remind her there is more than poverty and abuse; hint at a whole world of possibilities.

There's running away from your responsibilities and then there's cutting your losses – two equal but opposite readings of the same palm.

I'm too scared to review the past days' events. I don't know what they would show me. I fear they would reveal the face in the mirror, the face I glimpsed after I killed a man, the liveliest face I've ever shown myself, the brightest shiniest self I have ever had.

Basically the thing that worries me the most is that I know I should feel guilty and yet I'm glad that I don't. I feel all sorts of things about what happened, but guilt, shame, horror don't really come into it. I want to talk to someone about it, maybe get some counselling, tell someone everything there is to tell about MacDonald, the blue Renault man, my year tutor – all the men who have hurt me or upset me or deliberately treated me badly because of my sex. Somehow it has all become connected, jumbled up in my mind, and I feel as if I have managed to draw a line under all that unpleasantness. I think that if I could just explain it properly, I would be able to move on now.

But I have to contain the desire to explain, keep the surface as untroubled as possible. Put on an unconcerned face and face JJ with it.

Another evening, then, and this time the pager is off and Margaret is out. It is just me and JJ sitting on the squashy sofa, almost touching but not quite. We don't speak for a while. We know this is going to be an important conversation and neither of us knows where to start. It is like the beginning of a martial arts contest, where the first person to make a move will probably lose. I'm better at reacting than starting things off, and we both know that if either of us loses, we both do.

JJ looks at me and I can see my wry smile reflected on his face. There is too much knowing between us. I still can't think of anything to say, so I curl myself around and into him, so that we are closer together but the eye contact is gone, and I can feel the strangely familiar impact of his body against mine unsettling us both.

Typical male, I think, leaving it to me to get

things going. I look up at the ceiling, which is OK in the fading light, but I know it could do with a couple of coats of brilliant white. 'I'm thinking about taking a break of duty, doing a bit of travelling,' I say as casually as possible.

'Send me a postcard,' he says, settling an arm round me and shifting deeper into the sofa, 'if you're sure you really want to go.'

'I have no patience left for work. I'm all out of compassion and can't seem to fake an interest any more. The cat won't miss me. Candy's getting better all the time. I need some space, I need some light, I need some air and I can't seem to find them in London.' I want him to persuade me to stay. I want him to argue and tell me he can't live without me for even a week longer.

JJ takes a minute to think about things.

'Lou, I want you to stay. I want you to stay with me. I want you to stay because you want to be with me, and I don't understand why you want to go away. Take a break of duty, sure, or some unpaid leave if you've run out of holidays, but leaving the country is a bit too dramatic – come and stay at my place, get some country air. I know you've had a hard couple of months but isn't everything sorted out now?'

We are getting nearer the point now and I have to look at him again. His face is serious, hazel eyes clear and earnest. I've never seen anyone who looked more trustworthy, more honest, more deserving of love. I reach out and touch the side of his face, where I can see ginger stubble starting to show on his jawline. Even before I say anything I can see from his reaction that he has interpreted this gesture correctly. I don't know where it came from – some film or other, no doubt – the last tender touch of a mother whose son is going to war, the wife whose husband has just been diagnosed with an incurable and painful disease, the lover saying farewell to a partner setting off to seek his fortune. It is loss, love and regret all in one, and I didn't even know myself until I did it that I couldn't just stay with JJ and live happily ever after.

'What did I do?' he asks and I struggle to find a reason. 'Is it to do with the murder squad, the investigation?'

Of course it is, what else could it be? JJ destroyed a statement because he loved me, to save me or to save me from hassle. He may or may not have realised the full implications it contained, he may consciously or unconsciously have rejected or accepted those implications – I can't ask him. Whatever his reasons, he got rid of the evidence. I always thought he was the perfect policeman. The perfect man. The perfect man for me. But he wasn't; he isn't. Would he have been, if he'd let things run their natural course? Well, no, obviously that wouldn't have worked either. But I can't help feeling let down by him, basically, and as I think it through it starts to make sense to me. Don't think I can explain it to him though. But he is still waiting for an answer.

'JJ, the murder case isn't the only thing going on in my life right now,' I say, and I can tell he knows I am being evasive. We both did the same interview techniques course – both 'extremely competent', as I recall – we have been close friends for years and we've been moving towards an even closer relationship for the past weeks. I know that the way I'm holding my head, my voice and movements, the way I'm choosing my words, everything about me tells him I'm not being entirely open. I can't say, sorry sweetheart, but you're just not perfect ...

So I take the easy way out and kiss him instead. Relax into him so that we're touching all along the length of our bodies, one hand on his neck, the other between his hip and stomach. He's not easily distracted, although he does kiss me back, wrapping both arms round me. Not hard enough to cause the breathlessness I feel, though. But he raises his head away from me and asks me again.

'Is it something to do with the murder investigation?' Still a serious face, although there's a slight flush now along his cheekbones and his eyes are wider than before. His voice, however, is as steady as ever. 'Is it to do with the statement I shredded? You think I did it because I thought you were involved.'

I snuggle closer and lick his neck, breathing in his smell and tasting his skin.

JJ continues. 'Well, I did think you might have been there and that's why I did it, OK? I could just picture you being there that afternoon, if you left the office a bit early or had a meeting over the road or something. And you do talk to the weirdest people, and someone would have told you there was a body in the alley, and maybe, I dunno, at the end of a long day maybe you just didn't have the energy to deal with it. I mean, everyone turns a blind eye now and then, God knows, not to things like that, but you've never played by the rules exactly, have you? I think you had enough on your plate, needed to get home and just thought, well, why should you get involved? Call out SOCO and wait for uniform to turn up – he'll still be dead in the morning – that sort of thing. Oh, I know it is breach of duty or neglect of duty or just not doing what you should, but surely you know none of that matters – it doesn't affect how I feel about you.'

I've managed to position myself under his chin where he can't see my face and I'm listening hard and thinking fast. So here we are, then. I know what he knows and what he thinks he knows. I know that he loves me because I don't play by the rules, because I take risks and get away with things that other people don't. He thinks I have just been the same as usual, only more so, over the past few weeks. I know that I love him because he always does the right thing, because he is, old-fashioned as it may sound, true and worthy and good.

Only this time he isn't; this time he's changed because of me. And because he has changed, I can no longer love him as I did before. Never realised I was such a perfectionist. I can't work out if this means I can't love him at all.

In the meantime I will continue to press myself against his warm and muscular body. After all, I've been fantasising about this body since I first met JJ at training school. Used to think he was too good-looking for me.

I'm still not talking and he seems to realise this is not the moment to insist.

Some things are better left unsaid.

A useful piece of advice my mother never gave me.

Action plan – appropriate, achievable, measurable

NB: HOMICIDE ACT 1957, ESP. S.3

Obviously life is simpler if you can avoid killing people, but if you absolutely must, make sure you're really upset at the time – why accept full responsibility if you don't have to? You have to get life if you murder someone, but on a manslaughter charge, a sympathetic judge is more than likely to let you off on time served awaiting trial, or a couple of years' conditional discharge. However, it is better not to get caught at all.

First thing I did was go on holiday with Margaret, to a sunny white villa with a bright blue pool in the south of France. Took rather more cash with me than is strictly necessary for a fortnight's break. Left break of duty report for Julie to process for me.

I've told JJ where we are. He is not the perfect policeman, that's for sure. But he's a lot closer to my perfect man than any other man I've met. I hope he understands the trust I have in him, the belief I have that he will see things as I do.

I hope he phones.

I really hope he comes out to fetch me home. I haven't exactly covered my tracks and he is a detective after all. Can't believe I'm going to end up waiting for some man, after all these years of independence I'm ready to offer someone everything I am, my freedom and my life.

Actually, the very first thing I did was ask Margaret if she fancied a couple of months Thelma-and-Louisa-ing but she turned me down. So that left JJ as the only other possible co-adventurer.

I really hope he phones.

But then, I guess, if he doesn't, well, he's obviously not the man I want him to be, not the one I need, if indeed I need one at all. 'The perfect lover's never there and if s/he was s/he wouldn't be (and neither would you).' Oh sure, I'm more outgoing and relaxed being part of a couple. I like to know where the next shag is coming from, I like the security that comes with it, and perhaps most importantly I like knowing that everyone knows I'm with someone so they'll leave me alone. But I certainly don't need it.

I hope he phones. No, I hope he comes. Just turns up. Shadow falls across the page, I look up and there he is; or we stagger in from the bar and find lamps lit and music on. I've sent a couple of postcards. Couldn't find any saucy seaside ones, sadly.

Hey, at least I'm out here going somewhere, doing something. It's not like I'm sitting alone in a dingy flat painting my nails while I wait for my prince to arrive and transform my life for me.

I still think he'll phone.

The south of France is lovely this time of year. I may just stay a while longer. I wonder what will happen when I don't turn up to work, how long it will be before the unpaid leave, break-of-duty thing kicks in. I don't even know if they'll approve it – it is meant to be for some useful purpose, like having a child. Does having a good time count? Travel broadens the mind, and I'm learning a language. Surely that is enough. I don't think I want to go home, but you never know. Don't burn your boat if there's a handy dry dock, I say.

I sit on the beach here surrounded by contented warm people and can't think of any reason to go back to London – the grimy streets, the ignorant people, the endless succession of victims and criminals and fat policemen. Margaret has gone back to her fat policeman. I feel as if everything has been put on hold. I have stepped out of my life into a new bronzed skin. I think I might like it.

I got hold of an English paper the other day, several days old by the time it reached me, creased and battered but interesting reading, anyway. Funny how you get when you're away from home (you see, it still is home). I even read the sports page and the finance page, although neither's of much interest to me these days. Couldn't see anyone I knew in the births, deaths and marriages column, but came across an old friend in the home news section.

DEATH IN CUSTODY:

MURDER SUSPECT FOUND HANGED

An official investigation has been announced by the Press Office of the Chief Constable this morning after the discovery by detention officers of the body of Ronald Shakespeare in a police cell at Leeds Central Police Station. Shakespeare was wanted by the Metropolitan Police in connection with the murder of a serving police officer in London earlier this year. Few details have been released as yet but it is believed that the high-ranking detective officer was bludgeoned to death following an attempted robbery in the King's Cross area. Shakespeare, 58, was formerly known as Ronald Jacobs and had served terms of imprisonment for offences of assault and indecencies with children in London and Manchester. Witnesses who saw Shakespeare's arrest yesterday at a city centre pub following a disturbance state that he was drinking heavily all afternoon. It is believed that he was seen by a police doctor on arriving at the Central station but further details remain sketchy at this stage. The murder case is believed to have been closed in the light of Shakespeare's death, which police are believed to be treating as a suicide. The Police Press Office will make an announcement at a press conference tomorrow. This is the eighteenth reported death in custody in Great Britain this year.

There you go, interesting reading, *n'est-ce pas?*

I didn't think he'd make it to court, somehow. There couldn't have been much of a case against him. But the case is closed, maybe I should go home – as soon as I find home, I'll stay there. For the moment though, it's onwards and upwards.

Had a letter from Margaret this week, poste restante and probably a week or ten days old by the time she got round to posting it. Not much news really. She's in love, whatever that means. It means that DS Andrews is moving in. They're letting the spare room to Steady's girlfriend who turns out to be called Rhiannon and seems to be Margaret's new best friend. Not that I care.

JJ has passed his Sergeant's Board and awaits a posting. I know he's not the perfect policeman everyone else thinks he is, and maybe he'll realise it one day. Doesn't look like he's coming to get me though. Maybe I'll go back and get him. Give it a while, see what the idea looks like a few months down the line. See if it really was love or just lust with potential.

Cat isn't pining away.

Josie sent a card to the house inviting me to her wedding, a month ago now. I'll send her a postcard soon, tell her I've left. Someone in my family should know.

From this distance, looking at my old life from outside, I wonder why I made such a big deal of it. Why the panic and worry. Even in the very worst case, where fingerprints and witnesses and everything else had put me in the frame, wouldn't I have still been OK? If I have convinced myself, surely a jury would have been a doddle. It would all come down to a matter of reasonable force, and when you fear for your life – which is, believe me, exactly what you must remember to make quite clear to the court – how reasonable can you be expected to be? I've always been good in the witness box. I have an honest face. You'd believe me. You might even like me. I reckon I could swing it. Obviously a tan wouldn't go down too well, but a couple of weeks on remand would sort that out, if the worst happened. Taking that view, why waste taxpayers' money on a trial? Not in the public interest. Chill out, let the fuss die down, out of sight and out of mind. Wonder if JJ has given up on me just because I kissed and ran. Maybe he's just more patient than I am. We'll see.

I think now that it is better to be a happy pig than an unhappy philosopher – better, not in any moral judgement way, but just because it is better. I think there is a happy pig inside all of us, even me. I think it'll come out now I've settled somewhere warm and got my breath back. I'm looking forward to it. Park my Land Rover at the seaside, kip in the back, work in a bar, get an all-over tan, drink beer and smoke dope for a couple of months.

Hot sun, cold sea.

I really think that might work.

Non-Home-Office-approved restraint techniques

So you want to know what really happened, huh?
Maybe you'd like a bit more excitement, perhaps a
daring last minute escape, a car chase, a brawl,
more detailed descriptions, more adult language,
some standard sex and maybe a bit of kinky stuff
too.

Tough shit.

Although I could do all of that if I wanted.

OK, so maybe I do want to talk it over, rehearse it,

see what it sounds like out loud. Here goes. Are you sitting comfortably? It is not a pretty tale.

Let's run through the known facts first. See what we know and what we've surmised.

Mr Suit, I called him at the time.

DCI MacDonald, Fraser to his friends, if he had any. Certainly not that many turned up at the funeral; not that many people voiced their concern or spoke up to defend his reputation when the rumours started flying. A tall man, slightly overweight, in an expensive suit, on a hot day in the city, smelling faintly of alcohol, apparently angry and obviously aggressive.

Last mentioned in life, dragging me by the elbow into an alleyway in broad daylight just off a busy road in the middle of rush hour.

Next mentioned as an unidentified body, the one in the alleyway, having been cleaned out, all property removed, a large male body. Identity announced at a meeting at which it is revealed that he died of head injuries, sustained cuts to the body and was found partially concealed under rubbish bags. Initial enquiries turned up no witnesses and the reporting officer suggested a robbery gone wrong.

Louisa Barratt, age thirty-one, five feet eight, slim-but-strong, irrational fear of large men, present at scene where Mr Suit is last seen alive and first found dead. Expresses some degree of upset behaviour; displays guilty knowledge by destroying clothing; does not report events to police at the time or in the following ten days.

Oh, isn't it obvious? Do we really need the sordid details?

Quite often in rape cases the jury are unconvinced by the victim's evidence. They want to see her break down in floods of tears, re-live the horror of what happened, show them how devastated she is. It is not exactly voyeuristic of them, it is basically due to their lack of understanding and specialist knowledge. Then they find themselves faced with a dry-eyed woman who recounts what happened as if it is a story she's heard, a play she's seen, instead of the most awful thing she has ever experienced. And they don't believe she's telling the truth, the whole truth and nothing but the truth. Surely if it had really happened as she says it happened, she wouldn't be able to talk about it at all. Has she no shame? No modesty? Talking like this in front of a room full of strangers ... she must be making it up.

Maybe she's making it up for revenge.

Maybe she's making it up for attention.

Maybe she's exaggerating because she's unbalanced.

Maybe she's just making a mistake.

Why isn't she more emotional?

In America, courts sometimes call expert witnesses who explain this behaviour, so common in women who are victims of sexual assaults and domestic violence. The expert explains that it is a classic way of coping, a distancing procedure without which the victim would not be able to go through the trial at all. Funny, I don't usually think of Americans as being particularly advanced but there you go. Here, in what we like to think is a civilised country, home of democracy and justice, no such provision is made.

So excuse me if I don't shed any tears here, won't you?

Did I tell you I'm a landlady these days? I thought about dividing up some rooms, filling the house with students but Margaret protested. She's still there with DS Andrews and Rhiannon, collecting rent and sending it out to me. Yes, I loved that house but it is only a house, after all, when all is said and done I've left more than that behind before now. I've paid the deposit on my Land Rover with the first month's rent. It seems like a reasonable swap, to be honest. I can live in it and it takes me places. And if I go home, it'll be ever so handy for those south London speed bumps. I'm heading south and east at the moment, but who knows where I'll go next?

By myself at the moment, thank you, but I might be joined en route. I don't know if he's given up yet, but I haven't. Think of it as a trial – if he comes, he's in. Although it is already hot where I am now, and where I'm going next it will be far too hot for someone with fair freckly blistering skin.

So there he was, Mr Suit, remember him? I do . . . dragging me by the arm and there was me trying to resist being pulled along towards the small entry alongside the Oceana Fish Bar, leaning back and dragging my feet but it wasn't working. I could smell him, sweat and alcohol and some sort of aftershave, strong enough smells to drown out the rubbish and stale food smells native to the alley. I was struggling as hard as I could, pulling away from him and trying to catch hold of something, anything to cling to to stop him dragging me further out of sight of people walking past, but he was much stronger than me, and although there were people only yards away they were all busily not looking, turning away, feigning interest in an advertising hoarding across the road or checking their watches. About twenty feet along into the entry and just around a dogleg corner he suddenly wheeled round and dropped one shoulder into my body, pushing me hard into the wall, a boarded-up doorway catching my right shoulder blade as I slid into the space it created behind me before thumping into the wall. I could hardly breathe, all the wind knocked out of me, and as I started to panic I found I was struggling to pull air into my lungs, my chest tight and unmoving and I couldn't speak, couldn't get enough breath into me to breathe out, I was swallowing air but couldn't force it into my lungs, and then it was worse as one of his large hairy hands tightened round my throat as the other tugged at my top, pulling the silk up to my neck and dragging my bra up with it. His face was an inch from mine and he was smiling. I was too close to see his expression, all I could see was his bloodshot eyes, pupils dilated so he didn't look human, but I know he was smiling, and still I couldn't quite believe this was happening. What did I do to make this happen to me? And then he was muttering, not so clever now, are you? Not so clever not so clever and my head was banged against the door behind me, three hard knocks, so that I could hardly see, and I was trying to hold him away from me with one hand while I hit out at his face with the other, first with clenched fist but that didn't reach so I tried again with nails outstretched to scratch his eyes, tear into his face but he was still smiling and too heavy for me, far too strong and I thought there's nothing I can do here, the more I try and get him off the more he's going to hurt me, shit I think he wants me to struggle so that he can really hurt me, but one of his hands was pulling at my skirt, a close-fitting skirt that he was having trouble getting up over my hips and he looked down momentarily and that was my moment to do something, I gasped in a huge mouthful of air and shouted some of it back out at him, not a loud noise but a start, and as he glanced back up I shoved the palm of my hand up under his nose and away from me as hard as I could, my other hand backing it up for extra strength and he let go of my throat and unhooked his fingers from my skirt and for a half-second he wasn't touching me at all, surprised by the strength I'd found to push him away, but there was still nobody around to help me and in the moment I could have tried to run he moved slightly round, cutting down my angle of escape and instead of trying to get past him I looked round on the ground for a weapon, anything at all I could use to hit him, club him, cut him with, and he knew what I was doing and he was smiling again, jumping forward to grab me by the throat again, bitch bitch you've asked for it now, fucking cunt, spoken so softly he could have been asking the time or where the bus stop was, choking me now with his elbow digging into my throat as his hand grabbed my breast and squeezed hard, twisting and pinching as his other hand snaked up my skirt, fast and vicious and I wriggled sideways, falling into the doorway again, taking some of the pressure off my throat but ending up down on one knee, skirt round my waist with the man standing over me, forcing the fingers of one hand into my hair, pulling it out of its plait and shoving my head towards him and starting to loosen his trousers with the other hand and I can't believe he's so sure of himself now he thinks I'll just give up, pulling my head towards him and fumbling and I'm up in no time, twisting out of his grip, knowing I must have hurt my head but not really noticing the pain, concentrating on a length of old lead guttering I'm gripping in both hands and I swing at him as if I'm playing softball, with all my strength, getting as much of a backswing as there's room for, legs apart for a firm stance, well balanced, and he's still got his mouth open and his fly half-way down when it hits him on the side of the head, he staggers sideways and moves as if to come to-wards me again and he must be dazed because he's saying, sweetheart, sweetheart, come here, come to daddy and he's not smiling any more but he is still coming at me and I hit him, shake my hair back out of my face and hit him again until he stops coming towards me, until I'm quite quite sure he's not playing dead, until he's stopped those awful noises and my arms are so so tired.

Then I look up along the alleyway and there's nobody around to help me. I could have been raped or killed, what's the world coming to? But he's still keeping quiet and he has finally stopped moving. I'm safe for the moment, and I lean over him and tuck him back in, do up his trousers for him, he looks so stupid lolling there like that, a child could walk in and see him . . . I start to brush some broken glass off him too, don't know how that got there, and find that some of the pieces are sticking into him and have to be tugged free, carefully so as not to hurt my fingers. That piece of guttering is lying untidily in the middle of the entry, someone could easily trip over it. I replace it where it came from and with very little manoeuvring it fits neatly back against the wall, shoved slightly inside the remaining solid piece.

I can hear street noises again now, buses

labouring along, shouts in the distance, and I am almost surprised to realise that the outside world is still there.

I look down at myself, tug my skirt carefully round so that the button is at the centre at the back, the small split, which appears to have lengthened a bit, also central. I settle my bra back to the correct position, shrug my shoulders a couple of times, feeling the strain in my upper arms. My throat is killing me. I twist round to brush as much of the muck off the back of my top as I can, finding a graze on the back of my neck that I didn't know I had. My shoes are also dirty, with that sticky black grime that collects in uncleared streets. I wipe them on a piece of plastic. Look for my bag and see it next to his foot; have to lift his surprisingly heavy leg by the trouser cuff to free the strap. Several deep breaths. Head aches, neck hurts, still having trouble breathing. Comb my hair with my fingers, notice that I've broken a nail, bite it to a neater shape, twist my hair up and replace the clip that's lying near his head. Almost didn't see it there and where would I be without my favourite, trademark silver hairclip?

Walk to the tube station.

Home.

Hot bath, cold beer.